AWAKENING DESIRE

There was a moment of silence, and he moved closer. "Carmel, charity or gratitude had nothing whatsoever to do with my wanting to be with you."

She looked up at him, startled. "I—" Her eyes caught his, and she lost all thought. The desire that glowed within his eyes turned her brain to pudding.

It wasn't a conscious movement that swayed her body toward his, that tipped her chin up to accept his kiss. He moved toward her, too, almost imperceptibly. His hands caressed her arms and pulled her closer. Then his lips touched hers like a whisper.

The kiss deepened, exploring, urgent, quickly turning fevered. Sensations whirled and skidded through Carmel, mixed with a sense of wonder. This couldn't be happening, this man couldn't be holding her in his arms, tight and hard like he meant it. His long, hard body pressed against hers, and his tongue lazily, intimately explored the recesses of her mouth. A slow, hard burn started somewhere near the pit of her stomach and rapidly worked its way south.

BOOK YOUR PLACE ON OUR WEBSITE AND MAKE THE ARABESQUE ROMANCE CONNECTION!

We've created a customized website just for our very special Arabesque readers, where you can get the inside scoop on everything that's going on with Arabesque romance novels.

When you come online, you'll have the exciting opportunity to:

- View covers of upcoming books

- Learn about our future publishing schedule (listed by publication month and author)

- Find out when your favorite authors will be visiting a city near you

- Search for and order backlist books

- Check out author bios and background information

- Send e-mail to your favorite authors

- Join us in weekly chats with authors, readers and other guests

- Get writing guidelines

- AND MUCH MORE!

Visit our website at
http://www.arabesquebooks.com

THE LOOK OF LOVE

Monica Jackson

ARABESQUE

BOOKS

BET Publications, LLC
www.msbet.com
www.arabesquebooks.com

ARABESQUE BOOKS are published by

BET Publications, LLC
c/o BET BOOKS
One BET Plaza
1900 W Place NE
Washington, D.C. 20018-1211

First Printing: December, 1999

10 9 8 7 6 5 4 3 2 1
Printed in the United States of America

To my friend, Greg Gunther,
whose support and caring has never wavered.

Chapter 1

"Don't stand there looking silly. Come up here, girl. Let me take a look at you." Carmel stifled a sigh and approached the old man.

He scrutinized her, then snorted. "Nice hair, even though you got it all pinned back. Wear it down tomorrow. Fine skin, I always liked that smooth coffee and cream color. Eyes are good, large and clear, long-lashed. Mouth well-shaped. From what I can tell of your bone structure, it seems all right."

He took a breath, and Carmel opened her mouth to tell him she wasn't interested in his assessment of her physical attributes.

"You've got such a pretty face," he said, shaking his head. "What a shame you've let yourself go."

Anger rushed through Carmel, but she took a moment before she spoke. Her nursing agency needed this case badly.

"Girl, you need to do something about that body," he continued, gesturing with his cane. "Food must get up off the table and run when it sees you coming after it. What you need to do is to push—"

"Dr. Reynolds. Please don't get personal," Carmel said in her calmest, most professional voice. "I'm not getting paid enough to be insulted."

Her face was bland, pleasant even. The only external sign of her inner agitation was the tightening of her fingers on the clipboard that held the paperwork she needed to complete for Dr. Marvin Reynolds's admission to the nursing agency.

Why did some people feel free to lecture strangers on eating habits? And have the nerve to tell her she's big, like she didn't know already? This old man might be senile, but he was working her last nerve.

"I'm Carmel Matthews, your nursing case manager." She held out a hand. He ignored it and stared at her.

"I was supposed to get a nurse. My son made special arrangements that I was supposed to have an RN. I don't need a case manager."

"I'm an RN, and I'm in charge of your private duty care. I'll be responsible for any problems that may arise, and all the other nurses will report to me. I'll also be doing the scheduling."

"So, when are you going to be working? That's what I'm paying you for, isn't it?"

"I am working for you. I'll usually be on day-shift duty during the week."

"Well, go get me a cup of coffee and be quick about it. Then I want my breakfast."

Carmel opened her mouth and closed it again. She laid her pen down on the clipboard. The man was testing her. If the agency she partly owned didn't desperately need this high-paying private-duty patient, she'd gladly refer him elsewhere.

"Your kitchen is that way?" she asked, her voice a little too sweet.

"I hope you got enough sense to find the kitchen, girl. Get yourself some food, too and join me. I don't like to eat alone. Get yourself some grapefruit, one hard-boiled egg and black coffee. I know we're supposed to provide meals for the nurses, but don't think you can eat us out of house and home. You're going on a diet when you work for me."

"My name is Ms. Carmel Matthews."

"I know what your name is."

"I'd thought you'd forgotten. You keep calling me girl. My name is not girl, it's Ms. Carmel Matthews. And my diet is my own business."

At least he had the grace to look slightly shame-faced. "I was trying to help."

"I don't need any help, Dr. Reynolds."

He eyed her up and down. "Looks to me like you could use a hand."

She'd have to disregard him. The man talked like he'd lost his mind some time ago, although there was no history of dementia. Jasmine, her best friend and business partner, had told her that old Dr. Reynolds was an MD of the old school, arrogant, high-handed, and probably impossible to get along with. Jasmine had been right on the money.

"No, I really don't need any help. I can find my way around your kitchen just fine," Carmel said as she strolled away. When she glanced back over her shoulder, the outspoken Dr. Reynolds stared after her with a disappointed look on his face. She suppressed a grin. The old man was frustrated because she hadn't given him the battle he'd been itching for. Yet. If he kept on needling her, she'd put a check on him all right.

She drew in a quick breath as she walked into the

kitchen. Gleaming stainless steel appliances, dark green granite counters and floors, rich wood cabinetry graced the room. Copper pots and pans hung over a center island with built-in appliances. Her dream kitchen. Dr. Reynolds was right about her knowing how to cook some food, and if she had a kitchen like this, she didn't know if she'd ever want to come out of it.

But something about this kitchen seemed new and untouched. No life, no love, no one bustling around cooking good, down-home meals. This lovely home belonged to Dr. Reynolds's son. He was also a doctor and divorced for several years. The son's ex-wife had left no stamp of warmth or personality on the elegant surroundings. Not that it surprised her. Jasmine had filled her in on the juicy details of the younger Dr. Steve Reynolds's recent divorce from Sienna Lake. Sienna was a poster child for today's black superwoman. She looked like she had it all—beauty, money, and a successful corporate career, even though the rich, professional, handsome husband was history.

From the photos Carmel had seen of Sienna, she didn't look like she'd ever lifted a perfectly manicured finger to cook a meal. Shoot, it didn't even look like the woman ever ate. She must have taken all the household help with her when she left, because on the phone Jasmine had told her that the only domestic help was a lone housekeeper.

From what she had seen so far, the home was spotlessly clean and flawlessly decorated, in spite of the lifelessness that pervaded it. It was a home obviously bought with a large family in mind. It seemed deserted, far too large for the two men who inhabited it.

Carmel shook her head to clear it from her musing. She'd have the same thing she put on his plate, fried eggs with a thick slice of ham, a couple of pieces of buttered toast on the side, coffee with cream and sugar. A hard-boiled egg and grapefruit indeed. The older Dr. Reynolds had to be tripping when he'd suggested that menu.

Barely an hour later, the old man's eyes widened when he saw the breakfast that Carmel had made for herself. She sat it down across from him. "Would you like some more coffee before I sit down and eat?" she asked pleasantly.

He scrutinized the plate Carmel had set in front of him. She slid into a chair facing him and picked up her fork. His eyes narrowed as he took in the food on her plate again. He opened his mouth to speak, but she held up her finger before he got the words out.

"You look like an intelligent man, Dr. Reynolds. I know I don't have to remind you that what I eat is my own business, and this meal is well within the contracted terms of meals that you're required to provide for your nurses." She took a bite of eggs, chewed slowly and regarded him with a look of long-suffering patience.

"Uh, uh, uh, it's a damned shame," he said, frowning.

Carmel raised an eyebrow. "No, I think the breakfast turned out just fine."

"You know that's not what I meant."

Carmel shrugged and cut a piece of ham.

"I expect to be called by name," he said suddenly.

"Of course, Dr. Reynolds."

"My name is Marvin."

Now Carmel lifted an eyebrow. Was the old man calling a truce? "You can call me Carmel," she said.

He snorted. "I was going to call you that anyway. What do these high and mighty nurses expect to be called anyway, nowadays? Some title like Great Big

Giant Nurse Matthews? Though in your case it would be true.'' He chuckled at his wit.

Carmel restrained herself from rolling her eyes. No truce, the man was incorrigible.

When breakfast was finished, the kitchen cleaned and dishes put away, she sat down to finish the admission paperwork. A key rattled in the front door and she heard it swing open.

''That's my son. You've heard of him, haven't you? Dr. Steven Reynolds,'' the older Dr. Reynolds announced, pride glowing in his face.

Of course, she'd heard of him. One of Atlanta's top plastic surgeons. Successful, moneyed, divorced, and—

''You must be the nurse taking care of Dad,'' he said, his voice husky.

And drop-dead fine, Carmel finished her thought. He'd entered the room as quickly and quietly as a panther.

''Yes, Carmel Matthews.'' She thrust the papers aside and stood, offering her hand.

''Don't let the old man scare you away. He likes to test out the ladies.'' Steve Reynolds smiled down at her, the corners of his eyes crinkling in his handsome deep brown face.

''Don't talk about me like I'm not here,'' his father said, grumbling under his breath. Then, he shot a glance at Carmel. ''Isn't she a fine-looking girl, if only . . .''

''Dad.''

''Okay, okay.''

Carmel, embarrassed, barely held herself in check.

Steve glanced apologetically at her. ''Pay Dad no mind. Since he has retired he's practiced being outrageous until it's an art form, and he's not about to give it up now.''

"I told you not to talk about me like I'm not here."

"Sorry, Dad, but you do it all the time."

The old man snorted. "Privilege of age. Have respect for your elders. I don't care how old you are. I'll . . ." He shook his cane.

"All right, Dad," Steve said. Then he winked at Carmel.

"I told her she can call me Marvin, as long as she stays respectful," the older man said. "Too many Dr. Reynolds in this house."

Steve grinned at Carmel. "I see you've got Dad under control," he said.

"You think?"

"He's a veritable lamb compared to his usual."

Carmel shuddered at the thought of what his usual must be like.

"Are you the one I talked to at the office when I arranged for private-duty nurses? You are one of the owners, right?"

"Yes, that's me. Jasmine Flynn and I started the agency about four years ago."

"You've got one of the best reputations in town."

"Thanks." Carmel felt breathless. Chill, girl, she thought to herself. Don't go off the deep end. You know there's no way—

He eyed her ringless left hand. "I see you're not married."

"Nooo, I'm not."

"No children either?"

"I have two children." She wondered what that had to do with anything. "I'm on call twenty-four hours a day if there are any problems."

He smiled down at her. "I'll be seeing you often. We'll have to go out and have a bite soon, talk about Dad away from his big ears."

"You got nothing to say about me," a mutter came from behind them.

"I've got to get back to the office. I just wanted to drop by and meet you." He smiled and turned away.

Carmel stared after him for a moment. He was a very nice man. That wasn't a glimmer of interest for her she saw in his eyes? No. It couldn't possibly be.

Chapter 2

Carmel collapsed on her living room sofa to recover from her first day with Marvin. Her daughter Melanie strolled into the living room with a handful of cookies in one hand and an apple in the other. "I'm going to basketball practice," she said.

Carmel nodded, slipping off her nursing shoe and massaging her foot. "Call me if you're going to be late for dinner."

Melanie had turned thirteen a few months ago. Carmel kept waiting with a sense of apprehension for the terrible teenage angst and rebellion she'd experienced herself to emerge in her daughter.

So far there was no sign of it. Melanie remained her well-adjusted, cheerful, busy self. Carmel crossed her fingers almost unconsciously, praying that Melanie wouldn't do as she had and have to learn hard lessons the hard way. She made pains to keep communication lines wide open, wanting to be the one her daughter came to with her hopes, fears and problems. So far, so good.

She wanted to be the type of mother for Melanie that her own mother hadn't been able to be for her. At thirteen, hormones had hit Carmel full force. She was the only child of a single parent, but at that time Mama had been preoccupied with a problematic boyfriend. Besides, Mama had never been an easy person to confide in. She saw everything as black or white, right or wrong, and children were to be seen and not heard.

Carmel had started running with a fast group of friends and experimenting with all sorts of new and forbidden things, including sex. She'd had Melanie when she was fifteen. Two years later her son Trey came along.

Time passed, and she and her mother were tighter now. Not that Mama still wasn't opinionated and outspoken, but she'd been there for her lately. Despite everything, she'd never let Carmel forget her own power to do what she needed to do. "You can do anything, girl. So, you've made a mistake or two. We all have. Just keep on going on and don't let nothing stop you."

And that's what she did. Her energies had gone where they belonged, to her children and the new business she started with her friend a mere year out of nursing school.

She'd told herself she had no interest in fooling with men, especially the caliber of the few she'd started to let get close to her.

Maybe it was simply her poor luck, but finding a man who had drive, ambition and who wasn't allergic to hard work seemed nearly impossible. It seemed the men she'd met were simply out for what they could get from her. She'd soon had enough of relationships based primarily on satisfying some man's needs, be it for food, sex or companionship. *Lady, you should be grateful I'm here* was the message she'd gotten from them.

Forget that. No, she'd decided early on that that wasn't what she needed or wanted, and she'd gotten her priorities in order. It had worked out. Her kids were healthy and happy and she was doing fine. She felt she'd accomplished something in life.

She rubbed her feet one more time and stood, stretching. Her son was holed up in his bedroom supposedly doing his homework. She'd bet money he was playing computer games rather than working on the sixth-grade American history he was having trouble with. She needed to go up and check on him. She picked her shoes up and walked softly up the carpeted stairs to his room. Her lips tightened as she approached his room and heard the telltale sounds of the computer game.

Then Carmel's heart softened as she watched him staring intently at the computer screen, his hand tight on the joystick. He was a handsome boy, passionate about things that interested him, and brilliant in math and science. He hated English and social studies, subjects that she loved.

"Trey?"

His head jerked up, and from his guilty look, Carmel could tell he hadn't finished his history homework. She waited to see what he would say.

"Uh, Mom. I was just taking a break." He closed the game and picked up his book, moving to the desk he used for studying. Carmel gave him a long look.

"I want to see that homework before you sit down to dinner tonight."

"Okay, Mom." He grinned at her and flipped open his book.

Her son thought he could charm his way out of anything, and the worrisome thing was that he usually could. But he was a good kid, like Melanie. Putting them first and foremost in her life was paying off.

Carmel went into her room to change her clothes. She neatly hung her nurse's uniform in the closet, a size twenty. It had never particularly worried her before. It was a fact of life that she was big like all the women in her family. She'd thought about cutting down and changing some of her dietary habits for health reasons, but it had always taken a back seat to whatever else that was going on in her life.

No matter. She was perfectly healthy. Her cholesterol, blood pressure and triglyceride levels were just fine. So what was she worried about? Surely not men. She had good friends, the nursing career she always wanted, her own business, a loving family and a home. There was no time or reason in the world to worry about men. She had no place for them in her busy life.

Carmel glanced out of the corner of her eyes at that nurse's uniform hanging in the closet while she pulled on a comfortable pair of sweats. Steve Reynolds was the reason that size twenty bothered her all of the sudden. Steve Reynolds and that look in his eye when he touched her hand. That look she didn't dare speculate what it meant. Or to dream about what it could mean.

Carmel had a flash of memory of how it felt to have masculine arms around her. She closed her eyes in momentary pain. She didn't cotton to the idea that there was a part missing in her life that she was afraid to face, or even had any idea how to begin to deal with. It had been four long years since she'd been with a man. She shook her head as if to clear it, resolutely ignoring the empty, dissatisfied feeling that filled her. Forget about it. She had things to do, she reminded herself on the way down to the kitchen to put dinner on.

Busily shaking pieces of chicken in seasoned flour, she couldn't shake the memory of Dr. Steve Reynolds. Her heart skipped a beat. Lord, the man was fine, although there was nothing pretty or boyish about him. He oozed masculinity with his nut-brown skin and rugged African features and eyes so dark they were almost black. He'd towered over her, a big man, although without an ounce of spare fat on his muscular frame. She looked down at her own body and sighed as she turned to the stove and pulled out the frying pan.

Steve Reynolds's ex-wife was gorgeous and slim as were the other women she'd heard he dated. Carmel had best face the fact that the man was out of her league.

Carmel was setting the fried chicken on the table as Melanie bounded in. "Smells great, Mom. I'm starving."

"How was practice?"

"Good." She reached out toward a drumstick.

"You know better," Carmel said. Melanie withdrew her hand. "We'll sit down and eat in a minute. Go see if your brother is ready to bring his homework to me."

Going into the kitchen, she pulled open the oven door and was reaching for the rolls when the doorbell rang, startling her. Her thumb touched the hot metal and she exclaimed, hurriedly pulling out the pan and setting it on top of the stove as the bell rang again.

She sucked on the side of her thumb as she pulled open the door to confront whoever was lying on the bell. Jasmine stood in the doorway, hand on her hip. "It's about time," she said.

"Don't make me curse you out, woman. It's been a rough day."

"I'd say. Looks like you've regressed to babyhood comforts."

Carmel pulled her thumb out of her mouth. "Please. I burned my thumb on the stove because of some impatient person leaning on my doorbell."

"That's a relief. I knew that case was going to be rough, but I'd hate to have my business partner crack up over it."

"That man drove me—" Carmel started to say, when Trey ran into the room and thrust papers in her hand.

"Okay, here's my homework. Hi, Jasmine. I'm starving, Mom."

She gave a cursory glance at Trey's homework. He always did a good job. Getting him to finish it was the difficult task. "Let's sit down to eat." She glanced at her friend. "Jasmine, you're eating with us, right?"

"Do you need to ask? My timing is perfect as usual."

The kids had finished eating and asked to be excused. Carmel and Jasmine sat at the dining room table, sipping coffee. "That was good, but then again your cooking always is. If you ever get sick of nursing, you should consider opening a restaurant."

"I almost thought I had one already."

"Touché. You know I'd starve if you didn't feed me. Do you have anything sweet?" Jasmine asked.

"I don't know where you put it," Carmel murmured. "I have a cherry pie on the counter."

"Mmmmm. You want a piece?" Jasmine asked, heading for the kitchen.

"Please. Heat it in the microwave and put a scoop of ice cream on top, will you?"

Carmel sipped her coffee. She was feeling a little edgy. Jasmine showed up regularly for dinner. She'd meant what she said when she remarked she didn't know where Jasmine put it. Jasmine was her height, but she likely outweighed her by over a hundred pounds. Carmel marveled at the unfairness of it. She'd swear Jasmine ate more than she did, never exercised and never gained an ounce. Jasmine, golden skinned and birdlike, had a deceptively fragile exterior. All of Jasmine's appetites were large and her girlfriend was as outspoken and tough as they come. She intimidated most women, men too, and had few close friends except Carmel. They went way back, and she knew the soft heart and tragic losses Jasmine's rocky facade hid.

Jasmine set the pie in front of her and refilled her coffee cup. "Thanks." Carmel took a bite of the pie and chewed slowly.

"And?" Jasmine asked.

"And what?"

"You are going to tell me about Steve Reynolds's home? Get any calls from throaty-voiced women? Silky lingerie lying around?"

"And to think I thought you were interested in the patient."

"I want to hear about him, too, but tell me the good stuff first. I've had a crush on that man ever since I saw his picture in *Atlanta Magazine*. Now that is what a real man is supposed to look like. He got it going on."

"I can attest that he's as fine in person as his photograph."

"You met him already? Lord, girl, why didn't you say so? Was he as nice as he looks?"

"Very much so. He said we'd be spending a lot of time together." Carmel hid her smile in her cup of coffee.

Jasmine sat back in her chair, "No, he didn't say that. Damn, I wish I could have taken that case."

"And if there was any way you could have, you would. Although your accounting degree qualifies you to fetch and carry as much as my RN does. The patient definitely doesn't need skilled nursing care."

"But the family wants it and, most important, is willing to pay for it," Jasmine said.

Carmel drummed her fingers on the table. "I wonder if there's any way I can convince the man an LPN or nursing aide would do?"

Jasmine frowned. "The agency could use the money, and the RNs we have could use the work. Skilled nursing cases are scarce now. Besides, Steve Reynolds said his father specifically requested round-the-clock RNs. And Steve Reynolds specifically requested you. He's paying top dollar."

"That case calls for top dollar. The elder Dr. Reynolds was unbelievably rude and obnoxious. I thought he'd get tired after a while, but he didn't let up on my weight for a second."

Jasmine gave Carmel a sympathetic look. "He was probably testing you. Exercising his old coot privileges."

"He exercised them so hard today, I wanted to take that cane of his and knock him upside the head."

"I don't believe you said that, Ms. Florence Nightingale."

"We're going to have to pay the special care differential or we're going to have hell keeping nurses on that case. I'm going to have to tell Marvin Reynolds's son that we are going to have to bill the higher rate tomorrow."

"I hope he doesn't take his business to another agency."

Carmel shrugged. "To be perfectly honest, Jas, after today I don't really care that much."

"That bad, huh?"

"That bad. And without the excuse of being either crazy or senile. He's got every marble in place. The man simply lives to torture nurses. He actually told me a nurse's place is on her hands and knees on the floor with the mop water."

"He said that?" Jasmine shook her head, a look of worry crossing her face. "Elaine called in and I replaced her with Lenore on night shift."

"Oh, no," Carmel whispered. "Lenore will cuss that man out so bad he might call 911."

"Thank God, it's your turn to be on call," Jasmine said.

"Thanks for your support and sympathy," Carmel said dryly.

"Any time." Jasmine took a large bite of cherry pie. "This is really good. The store-bought pie crusts are never this light and flaky."

"I can show you how to make them."

"Surely you jest."

"You ever set foot in a kitchen, Jasmine?"

"Sure. To open the microwave and put something in."

Carmel chuckled, then sobered, thinking about Marvin Reynolds. "I'm worried that he might fire us and get another agency after a shift with Lenore. We do need this case. Maybe I should go in tonight."

"We don't need it that bad. If things don't turn around soon, one case isn't going to make a lot of difference."

"I thought you said the cash flow was getting better."

Jasmine shook her head, her eyes on her plate. "I got the news about our last appeal on the Levitz case."

Carmel laid down her fork. "I can't believe you didn't tell me as soon as you walked in the door . . . Oh, no, you're saying we lost, aren't you?"

Jasmine nodded miserably.

"I can't believe it. I made sure all the i's were dotted and t's were crossed. Those bastards. Are you sure?"

"It's in black and white, Carmel."

"So, it's true that we may go under because the granddaughter took our patient to a bingo game."

"Medicare's last word is, 'documentation refutes homebound status.' Case denied. Finis. The End."

There was nothing more to say, Carmel thought. They had exhausted every avenue of appeal. They weren't going to get paid, and that was that. The agency would have to eat thousands upon thousands of dollars of salaries and equipment. It would break them. The beginning of the end.

Jasmine looked bleakly in the distance, and silent gloom enveloped them as heavy as a blanket.

Carmel got up for another piece of pie.

Chapter 3

The shrill cry of the phone cut into Carmel's sleep. She fumbled for it, and the phone clattered loudly to the hardwood floor. She reached and groped for the receiver in the dark. She grasped it and held it to her ear. "Yes?"

"Ms. Matthews, I'm sorry to wake you," the deep, rich voice of Steve Reynolds echoed in her ear. That voice snapped her fully awake, her pulse starting to race.

"That's fine. What's wrong?" she asked with a sinking feeling.

"My father is insisting that you come out immediately and replace the night nurse. It appears as if they had an . . . altercation."

Carmel bit her lip. No need to ask the problem. With Lenore on duty, she could guess. "I'll be there as soon as I can."

Mama would come over to watch the kids. Jasmine would come in a pinch, but the unspoken agreement was that Mama watched the kids while Carmel took care of work-related emergencies. And this definitely sounded like an emergency.

When Carmel pulled up in front of the circular drive of the Reynolds house, Lenore stood in the front door with her arms folded. Carmel sighed inwardly at the pissed-off expression on Lenore's face. She looked like she had let Dr. Reynolds have it, and if she had cussed out a patient, Carmel couldn't use her anymore. That would be a shame, because despite her temper Lenore was one of the best nurses she had.

"That man needed to be cussed out," Lenore said as soon as Carmel got within earshot.

Carmel's heart sank. She looked at Lenore wordlessly and lifted an arched eyebrow.

"Don't look at me like that. I didn't cuss the old coot out, I just said he needed it. When he told me to get out of his sight, I just said, 'Thank you, Jesus,' because I was praying for something to get me away from that man before I—"

Carmel spied Steve standing in the living room looking toward them with interest and hoped he couldn't hear Lenore. "I'll give you a call later," she said.

"I hope you have more work than you have had lately. Another agency offered me a case, but I like working for you, but unless you can keep me busy . . ."

"I'll see what we can do tomorrow."

Lenore shrugged and lifted the strap of her bag over her shoulder. "Good luck. You're going to need it."

Carmel met Steve's eyes. "That I am," she murmured under her breath as she moved toward him.

* * *

The woman took his breath away, Steve thought as he watched her move gracefully toward him. Carmel Matthews was outrageously beautiful, with a feminine face, ridiculously long lashes, cupid bow mouth, and large expressive brown eyes that floored him when he first met her. Then he was impressed with her quiet poise, competent manner and the deft way she'd handled his admittedly impossible father. But her body . . .

She drew close, a touch of anxiety on her brow. "How is your father?" she asked.

Her scent assailed his nostrils, a faint whiff of vanilla and musk. Her body was the icing on the cake. She had full, straining breasts, hips he'd love to sink into, and a curved, soft belly, not taut and hard like his. Her thighs looked like they held a feminine softness he'd love to have wrapped around him. And her rear, the thought of such voluptuous deliciousness made him want to . . . Steve groaned mentally and put his hands in his pockets. At four in the morning, his defenses were low.

"Dr. Reynolds?" she said.

The touch of anxiety in her voice had turned to worry, and Steve hurried to reassure her. "Dad is fine. In fact after raising much hell, and getting me out of bed, once I told him I called you and you said you were coming in, he went back to sleep."

"Did our nurse do anything that disturbed you?"

"No. I think for once Dad didn't get the last word, and he threw a fit."

"Hopefully your sleep won't be disturbed again. Of course, I'll replace her on this case."

"I'm in surgery today. I need to be at the hospital by 5:30, so I'd be up anyway. No, Dad disrespected her, and I apologize for his behavior. If she's willing to put up with him, there's no need to take her off the case. Barring utter disaster, the next time Dad throws a fit, I'll throw a pillow over my head and let them work it out."

A tiny smile crossed her beautiful face. "I know Lenore well. She's an excellent nurse, but her temper is more than a match for your father's. You might regret you said that."

"I meant it. It's time Dad learned that he can't treat nurses any way he pleases."

Her smile broadened and her warm brown gaze met his. Steve's breath caught in his throat. "We'll see," she murmured, and started to turn to leave.

"Please, have a cup of coffee with me before you go up. Dad probably won't wake up for hours."

She hesitated, and turned back, their eyes meeting again. His next heartbeat was minutes long, the air thickening, making it hard to breathe, tension building between them, almost visible in its intensity. Steve's head bent toward hers, her perfect lips beckoning him to cover them with his own.

She stepped back. "Um. No. I better go, um, go get to work." She fled, leaving a whiff of vanilla in her wake.

Steve took a deep breath. Get a grip, man, what was wrong with him? It wasn't like him to make a move like the one he very nearly made on a woman he barely knew. The woman worked in his home for God's sake, she'd shown no overt sign of interest in him. What was wrong with him? If he'd followed through with his impulse, he couldn't have blamed her if she'd quit and slapped him literally, then figuratively with a sexual harassment suit.

He shook his head to banish the memory of Carmel's moist lips. He'd blame the uncharacteristic weakness on high morning testosterone levels. He poured himself a cup of black coffee in a travel mug. Maybe he'd head on over to the hospital a little early this morning and get to work. Steve grabbed his keys and headed out the door, still shaking his head. It wouldn't happen again. He'd be professional and polite—at least until she clearly let him know that she wanted more. He hoped it wouldn't take her too long.

Carmel splashed cool water on her face in the upstairs hall bathroom. She almost stroked out merely standing close to that man. It wouldn't do, wouldn't do at all. Her out-of-control hormones had to get in line. A crush was out of the question. She didn't need it, couldn't afford futile yearnings and useless dreams about Steve Reynolds. She had to be professional, to face reality. Her silly imagination was running wild. She'd thought he was going to kiss her. Yeah, right. In her dreams.

She took a deep breath and pulled herself together. Walking soundlessly into Marvin's room, she glanced over at his chest moving with deep, regular breaths. Steve was right, he wouldn't wake for a while. She walked over to the window and pulled the drapes to let the starlight in. She heard the rumble of a car and looked out the window in time to see Steve's sleek black car pull off.

Maybe she would go down and have a cup of that coffee. The glowing hands of her watch pointed to 4:35. It looked like it was going to be a mighty long day.

"I want that woman fired from the agency immediately. Is that the type of nurse allowed to work nowadays? No wonder medicine is going to hell in a handbasket. In my day nurses knew their place. We didn't put up with that sort of back talk. No, she would have—"

"Marvin."

Steve's father cast a baleful glance toward Carmel. "In my day, nurses also knew not to interrupt their betters."

She bit her lip to stop the quick and sassy retort that wanted badly to pop out of her mouth, and Marvin took that for contrition.

"That's all right. I know you didn't mean it. Sometimes you act like you got some sense. Half these young women act as if wolves raised them. No sense, no manners."

He took a breath, obviously going to continue with his rant, but Carmel grabbed the opportunity. "Do you want a cup of coffee before I help you bathe and get dressed?"

Marvin looked at her like she was out of her mind. "The day I let you help me take a bath is the day before I hope they put me six feet under. Get on, woman. Go down to the kitchen to start my breakfast."

With relief Carmel turned to head downstairs.

"Make me some fresh cinnamon rolls," he ordered.

Carmel restrained herself from rolling her eyes and added baking to the repertoire of nursing skills this case demanded.

The aroma of cinnamon filled the house by the time Carmel heard the rap of Marvin's cane beckoning her to the dining room.

She carried his plate in, graced by two huge, luscious-looking cinnamon rolls. They tasted good, too. She'd already had a couple herself.

"Well, get your plate and sit down, too. Don't just stand there towering over me like some fool."

Wordlessly, Carmel turned and poured herself a cup of black coffee. It was going to be a long day, she thought again.

Marvin grunted in approval when he saw that she only had a cup of coffee. "So you finally decided to put yourself on a diet. About time. You'll never get yourself a man looking like that. Why, I'd think twice—"

Carmel sat her cup on the table hard, coffee splashing over the edge and spreading toward Marvin's plate.

"Be careful, girl. Hurry up and get something to clean your mess up."

Carmel ignored the spill. "Dr. Reynolds, I have something to say that I'm only going to say once." She spoke in slow, measured tones.

For once the old man was silent.

"If you ever refer to my weight again, in fact, if you ever make any personal comment about me unrelated to my work duties, I'm going to walk out of here, and I won't be back. Am I clear?"

He sputtered.

Carmel pushed her chair back and started to get to her feet.

"I understand you," he murmured before she'd made it all the way up.

Carmel dropped back in her chair. "And furthermore, that not only goes for me, but for the rest of my nurses. I spoke to Lenore on the phone a few minutes ago, and she told me what you said to her."

He looked a little shamefaced. "What I said was true."

"Nevertheless it was unforgivably rude to comment on Lenore's teeth, breath and the size of her derriere in the manner you did. You have full command of your senses and I won't put up with disrespect either to myself or to my nurses. Is that clear?''

Marvin stared into his plate. Carmel stood up. "I'll call your son to have another nursing agency on duty within the hour.''

"No. Don't do that," he said.

"Then what do you propose I do?'' Carmel asked, her voice cool. She knew the question was a loaded one, but suddenly she wanted away from this house, from this case. More than the elder Dr. Reynolds was getting under her skin. His son had brought needs and desires to the surface that she'd thought were long buried. Needs and desires that she had no intention of tolerating.

"I don't see why you're getting so het up. I don't mean you or your nurses any harm.''

"Disrespect is harm, Dr. Reynolds.''

"All right, all right. Since you nurses have such tender feelings, I'm sorry I trod on your sensitive sensibilities.''

A backhanded apology if she ever heard one, but she supposed it would do.

"Now, are you satisfied? Will you sit down so I can finish my breakfast in peace?''

Carmel sat down, hiding her small smile of satisfaction as she took a sip of coffee. She sat her cup down, gently this time, and wiped the spill away with a swipe of her napkin. "I'm not firing Lenore, and I'm not taking her off the case. She's a good nurse.''

He started to open his mouth, then closed it.

"I'm happy we understand each other.'' She stood. "Now that I've gotten that said, I'm going to go get my plate.''

* * *

When Elaine came to relieve her two hours early, Carmel could have cried with relief. Marvin wasn't the problem. He'd behaved almost like a human being since she'd set him straight that morning.

Carmel was exhausted from lack of sleep, and her nerves were taut from expecting Steve to walk in the door any minute. She didn't feel up to dealing with him in her unsettled state. She didn't want to analyze her feeling that she'd rather face a firing squad than him right now. There'd be time to think about it later, after she got the staffing straightened out on the case, took a long, hot soak in the tub and had a bite to eat.

She hurried to her car and had just opened the door when Steve pulled up in his black Mercedes 450SL. She closed her eyes momentarily when she saw him get out of the car and stroll toward her. She dropped her purse in the seat before she turned to face him.

"I didn't tell you this morning how much I appreciated your patience with Dad yesterday," Steve said, smiling warmly down at her.

She pushed her heart firmly back down where it belonged. "Thanks. He's doing fine, but. I'm concerned about how he refuses to allow us to help him bathe or dress. I'm aware that the reason you got nurses was because of the frequency of his falls, and if we can't monitor him . . . I'm afraid he'll fall again."

"I know how Dad is. You can only do the best you can do."

"Thanks. We will do the best we can."

Silence fell between them.

"I wanted to apologize also," Steve said.

Carmel glanced at his face sharply, alarmed.

He wouldn't meet her eyes. "What happened this morning . . . Well, it won't happen again."

She was confused for an instant before she understood. "That's my job, Dr. Reynolds. I don't mind having to come to work early."

He started to say something, then he stopped.

"Please feel free to call me at any hour for any concern," she added.

"Uh, thanks," he said. "I hope I won't have to do that."

Carmel smiled at him, her equilibrium restored. Then her smile faded. "I told your father I was keeping Lenore on the case this morning."

Steve grinned. "And you still worked all day with him?"

"He was ultimately agreeable."

"Remarkable. He really likes you, you know."

Carmel shrugged. "I'm not sure about that, but we seem to have gotten an understanding."

"Well, like I said, I'll let Lenore and him work it out among themselves. If someone calls you in the middle of the night, it'll be one of them, not me."

She felt herself leaning toward him, and she backed away. "I'd better get going."

"I'll see you soon," he said. He walked to the house with a long, easy stride.

Carmel looked after him. His statement sounded like a promise, rather than the empty courtesy it was. Problem was she wanted to see him tomorrow and the morrow after that. Her desire read false meaning into his words. She slid in the car seat. Get a grip, girl, she said to herself. He's not for the likes of you.

Chapter 4

When Carmel got home, Melanie and the boy next door, Dean, were huddled on the porch swing, deep in conversation. They didn't look up until they heard her footsteps approach.

"Hi Mom." Melanie looked startled and not overly welcoming. "You're home a lot earlier than you said."

"My relief came in a few hours early. Is Mama here yet?"

"Grandma called and said she had to go to the church, but she'd be here before you got home."

"All right." Carmel hesitated, wanting to question her daughter further, but not knowing what to ask. Her mother's antennae were telling her something was . . . not right. She had no idea what the matter was. Dean and Melanie had been sitting on the front porch talking instead of in the bedroom with the door closed. Trey was almost certainly holed up in his room with his computer, not doing his homework.

"Dean finally talked me into joining the soccer team," Melanie said.

"We needed some decent players on the girls' team. All the rest of the girls are so stupid about sports. They don't have it together the way Melanie does," Dean said.

Melanie beamed.

"Are you certain you're going to have the time to keep up on your schoolwork?" Carmel asked with a touch of concern. "Remember how we talked about if your grades slip, some of the sports have to go."

"I'm doing okay, Mom. It's no sweat."

Carmel ran a hand over her daughter's hair, neatly pulled back into a bun. "Okay, pumpkin."

"Mom, please," Melanie groaned. "I told you not to call me pumpkin anymore."

Dean stood and ran down the porch steps. Melanie started after him, then stopped and looked back. "I think Trey is sleeping," she said. "He said he was tired and didn't want to be bothered." Then she bounded after Dean without a backward glance.

Carmel watched as they ran toward Dean's backyard. Dean and Melanie had been best friends ever since they moved into the Decatur neighborhood three years ago. A sports nut like her daughter, he was a handsome brown boy with a ready grin.

On the way to her bedroom to change clothes, Carmel stopped in the kitchen to take the roast she'd prepared that morning out of the refrigerator and put it into the oven.

Then she threw her uniform in the clothes hamper. Every evening was the same, she thought. She hounded Trey to do his homework, then got dinner on while she caught the news or talked with Jasmine or Mama. After they ate, she'd spend some time with the kids, and then watch a little TV or read before she went to bed and got up the next morning to do it all over again.

Carmel knew she should be grateful for all her blessings, but she couldn't quell the pervasive feeling of dissatisfaction that filled her. She needed to do something more with her life. She needed, needed . . . She feared the gnawing emptiness within her, resenting the dissatisfaction that threatened to unsettle her appreciation for the life she'd worked so hard to build. She quickly pulled on a pair of jeans, firmly pushing the troubling thoughts and feelings away.

The delicious aroma of roasting beef, onions, potatoes and carrots had started to fill the house when Carmel got to the kitchen. Reaching into the cupboard, she got down a half full bag of Oreos and filled a glass with cold milk.

Twenty minutes later Jasmine was ringing the doorbell. Carmel was glad to see her, happy for the diversion from her melancholy thoughts. Jasmine got herself a cola from the refrigerator and sat down at the table watching Carmel beat furiously at a bowl of batter.

"What are you making?" she asked.

"Brownies. I'm surprised to see you out of the office so early."

"When Irma said she wished I'd take my evil butt home, I decided to do just that. When I got there, seeing all the laundry I needed to wash depressed me. I thought I'd take a nap over here while I waited for dinner."

"I wonder what it would be like coming home to a cooked meal once in a while?" Carmel mused.

A flash of guilt crossed Jasmine's face. "You're tired of cooking? I can take you all out to eat. Lord knows, I owe you."

"Thanks for the thought. But I like to cook, and

I don't mind you coming over to eat. It's just that I'm in a funk today."

"Why?" Jasmine asked.

"I don't really know." Carmel opened the drawer to get a spoon to scrape the brownie batter into the greased pan.

Jasmine munched on one of the three Oreos that were left in the bag. "That time of the month?"

"No. I think I'm in a rut. I need to do something different than what I always do, but I can't figure out exactly what."

"You can do that inservice on home respirators for the nurses that you've wanted to find the time to do."

"I don't mean work. It's something else. I've been feeling restless. Antsy."

Jasmine nodded sagely as she picked up another Oreo. "I know just what you need."

"And what's that?"

"You need to get laid."

Carmel rolled her eyes. "You think sex is the answer to everything. Well, it isn't. I don't need any such thing."

"If you say so, but I disagree."

"Disagree all you want. I know a man is the last thing in the world I need. I have enough to worry about."

"Which reminds me of the reason for my fatigue today."

"I don't think I want to hear it."

"Oh, c'mon, Carmel. I met a new man, and I want to tell you about him."

"What happened to Michael?"

"Nothing's happened to Michael. He's been superseded, that's all."

"Does he know?" Carmel asked.

"Not yet. But I don't want to talk about Michael.

I want to tell you about the new guy I met. Keith. He's unbelievable, we were up half the night talking yesterday."

"Talking?"

"Yes, talking. That's what's so unbelievable. I'd met Michael for lunch at Remy's, and my gaze locked with this incredible man who was eating alone. Michael had to leave for an appointment and I lingered over coffee," Jasmine said.

"You were out to lunch with your boyfriend eyeballing available men? Typical."

"Don't interrupt. Of course, Keith joined me. He's from Macon, and he's in town for business. He invited me out for dinner after work, and I couldn't refuse. This man is—"

"I know, incredible."

"Dinner was fabulous and the conversation even better. We must have told each other our life histories. When he asked me up to his room to continue our conversation, well, what could I say? I was ready. But he was for real, Carmel. We talked for hours; then he kissed me on the forehead when I left. Said he didn't trust himself to do more." She sighed in bliss and wrapped her arms around herself. "I think he's the one."

Carmel grunted.

"Ease up on that batter, girl, or you're not going to have any left to make brownies," Jasmine said.

Carmel looked down at the bowl, surprised. She had spooned out half the batter and eaten it without thinking. "Damn."

Jasmine sniffed the air. "Hmmmm. Is that the reason you're going to town on the chocolate?"

"What are you talking about?"

"I'd swear I smell something a little funny, and it isn't tobacco if you know what I mean."

Carmel stood stock-still and stared at Jasmine. "Really?" She sniffed, and did whiff a faint tang of something that smelled burned.

She swore and took off in long strides toward Trey's room. The windows were open and a haze redolent of incense hung in the room. The smell wasn't strong here, but he'd likely taken special pains. He sat at his computer intent on a noisy game.

"Trey." Her voice had come out sharper than she intended it. He swung around too quickly. She interpreted it as guilt and her heart sank. For God's sake, he was only eleven. "Why were you burning incense?"

He shrugged. "A friend gave it to me. I like how it smells."

She decided to take the direct route. "And I smell that something was burned in this house other than incense."

Trey looked at her, wide-eyed and innocent, all the child he was. "What do you mean?" he asked.

Suddenly flustered, she realized that sometimes the direct route might not be the smartest one. For some reason she was finding it difficult to confront her eleven-year-old son with her suspicions.

She sighed, almost imperceptibly. "Have you finished your homework yet?"

"Didn't have any today, Mom. They decided to give us a break."

"All right. Dinner will be on the table in an hour."

When she got back into the kitchen, her mother had arrived and was busily chopping lettuce for a salad. Jasmine stirred iced tea and met Carmel's eyes when she entered. Jasmine's eyes were full of concern and questions. Carmel gave a little shrug, and moved to hug her mother. "How are you doing?" she asked Mama.

"Pretty good. There's a to-do going on up at

church. The choir director resigned and the secretary
is threatening to quit."

"Political infighting?" Carmel asked.

"No." Her mother wiped her hands briskly on the
apron she'd put on. "Affair."

Carmel's eyebrows shot up. "No, you didn't say
that. Not old Mrs. Kendricks?"

"And that dirty old man?" Jasmine finished.

They all started laughing simultaneously.

"There are some things you don't even want to
picture in your head. Yes, it's quite a scandal though.
They want me to pick up some of the slack around
the church. I'm not going to have as much time to
look after the kids. But they're getting older now,
and I don't see that as a problem."

Carmel shifted uneasily. She didn't want the kids
spending a lot of time alone. Things were changing
so fast with them her head was spinning. She was
certain of one thing—they were on the threshold of
the inevitable innocence lost. She knew there was
no stopping it, but she mourned the loss of their
childhood already.

Chapter 5

Around ten the next morning, Carmel and Marvin sat in the den while the CNN anchor expounded in the background on the state of the economy. Carmel finished reading the editorial section of the morning paper and handed it to Marvin. She shook her head at his proffer of the sports section in return, and had just started the entertainment section when she heard a key turning in the door.

It must be Steve. The thought caused her adrenaline level to shoot up. Then a brisk click of high heels on the marble flooring of the foyer sounded, and Carmel started to rise, puzzled.

"Sit back down, it's Donna. I told that woman she could knock like everybody else, instead of waltzing into my—"

A thin, elegant-looking woman in a beige suit strode briskly into the room. She looked to be in her fifties, with rich pecan skin and auburn-tinted hair coiled in a French roll. She stood before Marvin with her arms crossed and her foot tapping the carpeted floor impatiently.

Words poured out of her like a broken faucet. "I must speak to you about Steve. He's told me he won't be coming to my annual Halloween party because Sienna will be there. I want you to talk to him. I'm counting on him to be there and he's being totally unreasonable. I can't get anywhere with him, you know how stubborn he can be . . ."

Marvin groaned, then heaved a loud, long-suffering sigh and folded his paper noisily.

The woman's words trailed away. "Well?" she asked him. Her eyes flicked to Carmel. "And why are you here?"

"The question is why have you traipsed in my house acting like you have no more sense than an ill-bred sixteen-year-old?" Marvin asked the woman. "I told you not to use that key Steve gave you."

The woman opened her mouth and shut it again with a look from Marvin.

"Why are you coming to me running your mouth about some foolishness without speaking first?" he continued. The flow of Marvin's words resembled a fire hose on full force rather than a faucet, Carmel observed.

"And don't you ever, ever ask someone sitting in my house why are they here, when that's the question you need to be answering," he continued.

Ruddy twin flags, visible even through the woman's dark skin, burned on her cheeks. Her eyes narrowed and lips thinned as she stared dangerously at Marvin.

"Carmel, allow me to introduce you to this woman who interrupted our peace," Marvin continued. "I apologize for her rudeness. This is Donna Graham, Steve's mother, and much to my great pleasure, my *ex-wife*. Donna, this is my nurse, Carmel Matthews."

Donna shifted her glare to Carmel, eyeing her up and down and dismissing her in that glance. "Are you quite done?" she asked Marvin.

"Quite." Marvin leaned back into his chair.

"Why do you have a nurse here? Are you ill?"

"Don't go getting your hopes up, Donna, I'm no sicker than you, which admittedly isn't saying much. No, this is Steve's idea. I lost my balance and fell and he decided I needed someone with me. Since he insisted, I insisted he do it right. RNs around the clock." Marvin grinned at Carmel.

"I see you're still determined to waste all the money you can," Donna said. "My regret is when you fell you didn't hurt yourself badly enough to really need a nurse."

Marvin rolled his eyes. "She's full of laughs, isn't she Carmel?" Then his smile faded as quickly as it came and his eyes became as cold as chipped hard coal. "Is that all you came to say to me? If you can't manage to speak to me with courtesy, you can turn your narrow butt around and march right on out that door."

"Good morning, Marvin, how are you?" Donna drawled, a sarcastic edge to her voice.

"I'm doing quite well. Have a seat and tell me what brings you here this fine morning. Maybe Carmel wouldn't mind offering you some coffee?"

Carmel stood, relieved for an excuse to get out of the room. "May I get you something?" she asked.

"No," the woman said, not bothering to look at Carmel. "Marvin, have you finished playing your games, so I can finish telling you about Steve?"

"As if I could stop you."

"He said he wasn't coming if Sienna would be there. Which is ridiculous. Sienna must be there, people come just to meet her. My daughter-in-law

would be crushed if I told her she had to stay away
from my party."

"Your ex-daughter-in-law. Of course it wouldn't
occur to you that Steve wouldn't want a repeat of that
debacle Sienna pulled at the last get-together you
hosted?"

"That was a joke. Steve usually has such a sense of
humor."

"The joke was in very poor taste."

"I think he was upset because of that man Sienna
brought along last year," Donna said.

"If you think that, you've lost the last noodle you
had. Maybe you got your hair pulled back too tight
to think straight."

Carmel bit her lip to keep from chuckling at the
aghast look on Donna's face. Marvin certainly had
an antagonistic relationship with his ex-wife. Then
again, Donna felt comfortable enough to walk into
the house to talk about Marvin, hoping that he could
influence their son. Interesting. She was dying to
know exactly what Sienna did to Steve, but didn't
dare ask.

"You never change," she hissed. "I don't know
why I bother to visit you, to make sure you have what
you need."

"Since it's obvious I have everything I need, I don't
know why you bother to visit me either."

Donna's face tightened and she stood. "Tell your
son I expect him to be at the party, and I'll keep
Sienna in check to make sure there's not a repeat of
what happened last time." She turned on her heel
and marched out, head held high. The slam of the
front door as she exited reverberated through the
house.

"The day that woman left me was the happiest day
of my life," Marvin said. "She wouldn't stay home

and mind her own business if her life depended on it. All she did was run all around town, shopping and spending money and minding everybody else's business but her own. That woman clucks about folks more than a henhouse. I'm surprised somebody hasn't knocked her block off by now." Marvin took a sip of coffee and Carmel waited, hoping he'd continue. Maybe he'd get around to telling her what had happened between Steve and Sienna at that last party.

"Now don't get me wrong, she was fine as wine in her day. But those hot looks were as fake as her makeup. I can hear her whining now. I'm too tired. I got something else to do. I don't feel good. I got to make a phone call. I don't want to mess up my hair. Shoot, I'd be lucky to get me some once a week, if that."

Carmel couldn't help the laugh that bubbled up.

"It might be funny to you, but you never had to live with that woman. I pity the fool that married her after me. She's not stupid, she gave it up for a while to get him good and hooked, but then I can guarantee the well ran dry. By now, Gene Graham ain't getting—"

"Marvin, I think that's enough."

"Oh, excuse me. I forget your tender nurse feelings. Though it's beyond me how someone that can empty a nasty, funky bedpan or give an enema can have such delicate sensibilities."

The man was impossible. "I'm going to fix lunch. Is there anything in particular you want?" Carmel asked.

"Whatever you cook is all right. Be sure you make enough. Steve said he's coming home for lunch."

Her heart skipped a beat, and a mixture of apprehension and anticipation filled her as she headed for the kitchen.

* * *

"The girl can cook, can't she?" Marvin said to Steve. Then he shifted and cut his eyes to Carmel seated next to him. "I meant to say the woman can sure cook."

Steve looked up from his plate with a smile. "Yes, she can. Thanks Carmel, lunch was great. I may have to drop in for lunch more frequently."

Carmel controlled her facial expression, but the thought of Steve dropping in for lunch all the time shook her. The man made her nervous, uneasy . . . hot. "I'm probably not going to be here for lunch often. I'll be cutting my shifts short occasionally, and another nurse will be coming in to relieve me by noon. I need to spend more time at the office."

"I don't want any more nurses," Marvin said with a frown.

"You won't have. Elaine will come in earlier, and Lenore will be working twelve-hour shifts. The relief nurses will change, but your primary nurses won't."

"I don't like it. Why are you going to give that heifer more hours?"

"Heifer?"

"You know who I mean."

"Lenore told me you two were getting along well. And you've gone for four hours without complaining about her once."

"Humph. I guess I don't care if she has more hours, but those relief nurses drive me crazy."

"Not nearly as crazy as you drive them."

They glared at each other. Steve raised a disbelieving eyebrow when his father backed down and picked up his cup of coffee.

"I still expect you to manage my case, and that

means you need to come out and see how I'm doing personally," Marvin said.

There was only a touch of triumph in Carmel's grin. "No problem," she said.

"You sick?" Marvin asked.

"No, why do you ask?

"You hardly ate anything at all. That sure isn't like you."

It wasn't the first time Carmel had the impulse to wring Marvin's scrawny neck, nor did she think it would be the last. "We had an agreement on your comments about my food intake."

"I wasn't commenting." Marvin looked over at Steve. "Do you think I was commenting? I think I was showing concern over the state of her health. Sitting over there picking and plucking at her food, when any other time, you'd want to take the fork away from her and give her a shovel."

"Dad, you're out of line."

"Well, excuse me. And I apologize if I bruised your tender feelings, Nurse Matthews. Humph." With those words, he got up and marched into the den without a backward glance.

Steve met Carmel's eyes, amusement in his. "I'd apologize for Dad, but it seems as if you got him well under control."

Carmel picked up her coffee cup, hiding her discomfort at the unaccustomed shy feeling she felt. The steam mirrored the heat she felt rising under her skin. She wished Marvin would come back. "Your dad and I have come to an understanding."

"You're the first person I've seen get him in line so quickly. My mother couldn't even handle him half the time."

"I met your mother. She came by to visit with your father earlier."

Steve laid his fork down. "Oh, yeah? I wonder what she wanted from him this time?"

Carmel shifted in her chair uncomfortably, wishing she'd never brought the subject up. "She was discussing some party."

"I can guess that I was the topic of discussion." He sighed and ran his hand over his hair. Then, with a small shake of his head, he smiled at Carmel again, causing another flip-flop of her heart. "Thanks for the lunch. I enjoyed the food." His smile widened. "The company wasn't bad either."

Then he was gone. Carmel looked after him, then she sighed. The tough thing was that Steve Reynolds was such a nice guy. She could deal with drop-dead handsome, even scrumptious fine. Success, intelligence and creditworthiness were qualities she could take in stride also. But add nice on top of all that and the combination would jangle any woman's nerves.

Jasmine and Carmel had to let Irma go. There was no way around it if they wanted to keep their agency in business even a little while longer. Carmel sat miserably in the far corner of Jasmine's office. They both waited in silence and watched the minute hand move toward the twelve. Almost five o'clock. At the exact moment the hand stood perfectly erect, a sharp tap came at the door.

"Come on in," Jasmine called.

Irma walked in, a tiny frown on her face. She sat down in front of Jasmine's desk. "I have something to say first," she said.

Jasmine looked nervous.

"Sure," Carmel answered, primarily grateful that the moment was delayed a bit longer.

"I've decided to accept another job. I realized for

a while that you two were going to have to lay me off."

Carmel let her breath out slowly. Of course Irma would figure out what was happening and make sure her bases were covered.

A broad smile broke out on Jasmine's face. "That's wonderful." Then she sobered. "Of course we hate to lose you."

"Yes, we hated that we were going to have to lay you off. It was so hard. You've been with us right from the start," Carmel said.

"I'm going to miss you two," Irma said. "It's a shame things are hard now, you've both worked so hard. But I believe you will make it through this hard time. Just don't give up, never give up."

She dabbed at her eyes and stood. "I have to get home to watch my granddaughter tonight. Do you want two weeks' notice?"

"It's up to you," Carmel replied.

"I start my new job in two weeks, and I'd like some time off. Why don't I come in Monday to clean out my desk."

Jasmine nodded, and Irma left the room without a backward glance.

"Thank God she knew," Carmel murmured.

They sat there in silence. The atmosphere was full of unspoken worries. The company they worked so hard to establish, that they were both so proud of, was going under. It was unfair because they'd done everything right. The constantly changing government regulations and payments and the corporate giants who had no intention of maintaining a level playing field had crushed them. There was no way they could afford the equipment and training it would take to put in place the new documentation the government had demanded. They would be out of business and that would be that. It was only a matter of time.

"Let me take everybody out to eat," Jasmine said, finally breaking the silence.

"Thanks, but I don't feel like going out. I don't much feel like cooking either though."

"We'll order pizza."

"Sounds good." Carmel sighed heavily. "I need to get back home and check on the kids."

"Whatever happened with Trey and the suspicion of funny cigarettes? You never said anything."

"There was nothing to say."

"He denied it?"

"Not exactly . . ."

"Carmel! You mean you never talked to him?"

"He's just a kid."

"You know better than that. Kids his age are smoking crack and knocking off liquor stores. You'd better talk to him."

Carmel sighed again. "I know. I will. I'm just finding it difficult to find the words to discuss drug usage with my baby, my little boy. I wasn't ready for this so soon. Somehow 'just say no' seems a little trite."

"Isn't that a bunch of utter uselessness? But then again, look how the kids of the former first lady who pioneered that phrase turned out. That was one woman not too grounded in reality," Jasmine said.

"She didn't have to be. She had enough chutzpah, power and money to construct her own version of reality."

"And to take a long break at the Betty Ford Clinic if the construct crumbled."

Carmel chuckled. "I thought I'd open a line of communication with Trey before I started going and making accusations. Try to let him know he can tell me anything without a knee-jerk reaction. I think that was the problem when I was a kid. I was afraid to talk to Mama about anything because I knew she'd go off."

"That sounds like it makes sense. Good luck."

"I'd hoped I wouldn't need it, but thanks, because I know I will."

Chapter 6

Steve walked into the kitchen, weary at the end of a long workday. He stopped in the doorway when he saw Carmel staring out of the kitchen window into the night, a cup of steaming liquid in her hand. His father chuckled along with some sitcom laugh track in the den. He glanced around the spotless room. There was no evidence of the meal she'd cooked except the pots on the stove, silently awaiting his arrival.

He should clear his throat or something to announce his presence, but instead he swallowed and leaned against the doorjamb, watching her. She was unlike the other women he'd dated, slept with, married and thought he'd loved. He realized her body was outside the norm of what most of his friends would consider beautiful. But without a doubt, she was beautiful to him.

So much so that he couldn't question the physical

attraction she held for him. Instead he questioned his previous fixation on bodies that now seemed skeletal, and about as attractive as a starving Somalian woman seen on a television documentary. He questioned why he always ran with the other wolves in the pack and missed the attraction full-bodied curves and feminine softness held for him.

But it was more than just the physical. There was something about the very essence of her that attracted him like a bee to honey. He'd tested the feeling, and listened and observed her over the weeks. Her keen intelligence was obvious, her down-home common sense even more so. Everything she did was simply so . . . right to him. From the sound of her voice to the way she took no guff from his dad.

Suddenly Carmel turned and faced him, as if she'd sensed his eyes on her. "Steve . . ." she said, her voice trailing off, the question in it clearly audible.

He straightened. "I was just wondering what Joy cooked for dinner. Smells wonderful."

"I cooked. Joy took the evening off. I'm covering for Elaine, she had the flu."

"It's good to see you. I missed you."

She drew in a breath at his words.

Steve looked away, unaccustomed embarrassment heating his face. What had made him say that? How could he tell someone he merely knew on a professional basis that he missed her?

"Can I make you a plate?" she asked.

"Thank you. Would you keep me company while I eat? Sometimes I get tired of eating alone," he said.

She joined him a few minutes later and handed him a plate full of savory looking pork chops, macaroni and cheese, and greens. She could cook, and cook the kind of rib-sticking food neither his ex-wife nor the women he'd dated would touch in their misguided pursuit of thinness.

"It looks great." He bent his head in a brief silent moment of thanks and dug in. He hadn't realized how hungry he was, and a few minutes passed before he looked up at her again. She sipped her coffee, regarding his obvious relish of her food with a slight smile.

He smiled back. "Tastes great too."

"Save room for dessert. Cherry pie."

Sighing in bliss, he cut another piece of pork. "Your company is very easy. I don't feel the pressure to make conversation, which is a good thing since I haven't taken my face out of this plate of food since you set it in front of me."

She grinned at him, and the unexpected wattage almost slammed him back into the chair. "I put small talk on the same level as pro wrestling, caviar and cucumber sandwiches."

"And what do you have against pro wrestling, caviar and cucumber sandwiches?"

"Pro wrestling is fake and the men tend to be unattractive and not too bright. Caviar is fish eggs and looks and tastes it—need I say more? Cucumber sandwiches are simply a waste of bread."

Steve chuckled. "You left out small talk."

"An expenditure of good breath better spent eating."

He laughed out loud, enchanted. "You run a business, cook and keep my father in line. I think that and how you feel about small talk gives me ample reason to propose marriage."

Her smile faded, and a frown creased her beautiful brow. He could sense her pulling back, and he wanted to hit the side of his head with the heel of his hand. What was wrong with him?

"Don't tease me," she said, her voice low.

"I'm sorry. I was . . . joking."

She looked away. "Your dad seems to be steadier on his feet, but I'm worried about his appetite."

"Dad's never had a problem putting away food."

"He's losing weight. I'm trying to get him to make an appointment with his doctor, but—"

"I know. I'll talk to him, and if that fails I'll check him out myself."

Carmel smiled at him again and he felt as if the sun had broken across the sky on a dreary, cloudy day. "Your dad thinks the world of you. You can see his chest swelling when he talks about you."

Now it was Steve's turn to look away, embarrassed. "We've always been close. He does have another side to him other than the irascible, irritating one he favors now. In many ways we're very much alike."

He tried not to grin as Carmel's head snapped up, eyes wide. "Really?" Her voice dripped guileless incredulity.

"Really. Dad's having a great time pulling all the nurses' strings. It's good for him. He looks a good ten years younger nowadays."

"Good to know we're doing some kind of good at least."

He reached over and touched her hand. "You're doing a lot of good for both me and Dad. There's some life in this house now. It needed a woman's touch."

Did Steve just say he needed a woman's touch? Oh my, Carmel thought. She took a breath to avoid going into cardiac dysrhythmia. His hand still covered hers. She longed to snatch her fingers away as much as she wanted . . . She was afraid to allow herself to think of what she wanted from Steve Reynolds.

"You nurses have brightened up Dad as much as this place," Steve was saying. "That alone is more than worth the fees."

The place. He had said his home needed a woman's touch. As much as what she'd thought he said formerly disturbed her, she'd liked it better than the idea that he wanted to move some woman in here permanently to redecorate or something.

"Didn't your ex-wife decorate the place?"

"Sienna hired a decorator. She was hardly home enough to bother with the place herself."

Carmel didn't know what to say in reply, so she remained silent.

"You told me you had two children. How old are they?" he asked.

"My son is eleven and my daughter is thirteen." Carmel saw surprise in Steve's eyes, and waited for the inevitable comment that she didn't look old enough to have children that age.

"Your daughter is entering a scary age. Nervous?" he asked.

"Very." Carmel met his eyes. "I was fifteen when I had her. Like many teenage mothers, I want her to have more options than I had."

"You can only do the best you can."

"That's true, but I'm determined that my best be good enough. My children are the most important thing in my life."

"They should be."

"Actually, right now I'm more worried about my son than Melanie. He's entering a difficult stage, and I sense him pulling away. It's becoming hard to talk to him."

"That is a tough age. I remember that was when I

discovered girls. Before then I knew they existed, but frankly I didn't see the point of them."

"Not only girls, I think I worry more about the boys he's running with. There are a lot of things out there to worry about. I know it's silly, but sometimes I feel like I'd just like to never let them out of the house."

"I suppose that's understandable. A man in your son's life might help. At that point in my life Dad became more important to me, and Mom faded into the background."

"I think a male role model would be good for Trey. But he's only got me, and I can only give him my best."

The sound of someone clearing his throat caused both of them to look up in unison. Marvin stood in the doorway. "I came to get another piece of that cherry pie. I didn't know you were home," he said to Steve.

"Would you like some pie too?" Carmel asked Steve, standing up.

"I was counting on it," he said, that crooked, sideways smile of his catching her heart.

It was so easy to talk to Steve, to confide in him. She could hardly believe that she'd been telling him some of the fears she had concerning her children, fears she'd not shared with anyone. She could sense the care and concern emanating from him in an almost tangible way. By now from most men she'd have sensed disinterest or concern about what she might be wanting from them. Steve was different. He listened carefully to her words and responded to what she said, rather than what his ego may have thought it heard. He was very different. Better.

But were the undertones of interest she discerned in Steve merely wishful thinking? Must be, she said to herself as she cut two generous slices of pie, thinking of the woman he'd married, the other women she'd heard he dated before. Women who were nothing like she was. Any of that sort of interest she might think Steve had for her was nothing but wishful thinking. A touch of depression descended as she slid a third piece of pie on a plate for herself.

Chapter 7

"Mom, how do you get someone to like you?"

Carmel's head snapped up from the book she was reading at Melanie's question.

"I don't know if you can get someone to like you, sweetheart. They either do or they don't. You can't force affection."

Melanie sighed and threw herself on the couch. "Well, he likes me well enough, but not in the way I want him to."

Carmel laid her book aside. It was the first time her daughter had voiced any interest in boys or concern whether they liked her or not. She stifled a sigh. She knew the time was coming. In fact, it was overdue. "How do you want him to feel about you?"

"I don't know." Melanie sat up and wrapped her arms around herself. "I want him to think I'm beautiful, and that I'm a girl. I want to be like my friend Alexis. All the boys treat her like she's a princess or something."

Carmel moved next to her and drew her close to her. "Just be yourself, baby. It's more than good enough. The boys like you already, and that special boy will like you for who you are. You can't try to be someone you aren't."

"Dean is acting so silly over Alexis, and he's my friend. He's always been my best friend, but now if Alexis is around he doesn't pay any attention to me."

Carmel had hoped in the back of her mind that Melanie would have her first crush on a singer or movie star, someone safely distant and physically out of reach. But it looked like it was the boy next door, Melanie's playmate since they'd moved into the house three years ago.

She hugged her daughter in a sudden fierce hug, wishing she could take all the teenage angst ahead off her shoulders. It was a necessary stage, and Carmel could only be there for Melanie.

"Being or looking a certain way isn't the key, although I know sometimes it feels like it. Be yourself, and continue being a good friend to Dean. Girls like Alexis will come and go, but a good friend will always be there."

Melanie gave a reluctant nod. "I guess so. I just wish I was prettier . . ." The sentence trailed off.

"You are beautiful, sweetheart. Believe me, you are." Carmel wished with all her heart that her daughter would believe her.

Trey strode through the den to the front door.

"Where are you going, young man? It's dark outside," Carmel said.

"I'm supposed to meet my boys at the bowling alley."

"Excuse me? You're not *supposed* to do anything at this time in the evening but be at home where you belong. I know you haven't lost your mind to the degree that you were going to waltz out of this house without saying anything to me."

"Mom, I *have* to be there. They'll think I'm some sort of punk or something if I don't show up. Everybody else is going to be there."

Carmel frowned. "It doesn't matter how wild other people allow their children to run. You are not going out alone after dark and that's that. You can call them and tell them what I said. If somebody has a problem with it they can talk to me."

Anger glittered in Trey's eyes, and he wheeled stiffly and stalked toward his room. In a moment came a loud crash as he slammed the door to his room. Carmel started to rise and go after him, but then thought better of it. She'd let him cool off awhile, then she'd go and talk to him. Melanie was right on schedule to go crazy from the influx of hormones released at puberty, but Trey was way ahead of schedule. She'd thought with boys being delayed that she'd have at least a few years yet before he'd lose his mind, too.

Marvin crowed in triumph as he threw his hand of cards down and scooped up the chips on the table. "At this rate you are going to be paying me to work here."

"As long as the money isn't real," Carmel said. "Since poker is more of a game of chance than skill, I don't see why you get so happy when you beat me."

"Sour grapes," he said, grinning in satisfaction. "I must say I'm happy you didn't cut back your hours after all. All this winning puts me in a good mood, and work is good for you."

Carmel didn't keep working eight hours a day at

the Reynolds's house to lose at cards, or for the sheer joy of working. She worked for the money.

"I like your company, too. Unlike most women you know when to keep your mouth shut." Marvin shuffled the cards with a flourish and arched an eyebrow at her. "My son needs a good woman. Those hotties he's been dating ain't worth a damn."

"Hotties?"

"You know what I mean. You can cook, keep a clean house, keep your rear at home instead of running all over town. My son needs a woman like you."

Carmel felt her face flush with heat, and she longed to tell Marvin to shut up. But from past experience, she knew that was futile.

"You'd have to take off a goodly amount of that lard or he'll never look at you twice. Man's got to have a presentable woman he can take out to parties and such . . ."

Carmel stood up and walked toward the door.

"Awww, now there you go, getting mad. I was telling the truth, girl. You'd make a fine daughter-in-law if—"

Carmel closed the door firmly behind her, shutting out Marvin's words. She wondered if he had any idea how much they pained her. She was deep in thought when she ran straight into a hard chest. She slowly lifted her head, her suddenly jangled senses letting her know exactly who he was. Steve. He crept around like a cat. She never knew when she'd literally walk into him.

He'd wrapped his arms around her, and she became excruciatingly aware of her breasts crushed against his chest, his long, hard body against hers. Seconds felt like minutes and she tipped her head up to look at him. Their eyes met. Brown and brown mingling, like . . . "Coffee and toast."

Then realized she'd said the words aloud from the utterly baffled expression on Steve's face.

"Excuse me?" he said.

He hadn't let her go yet. She wished he'd let her go. She was finding it hard to breathe. "I wanted to know if you wanted some coffee and toast."

Now he looked puzzled. "No, but some lunch would be fine."

"Okay." Carmel fled to the kitchen. Steve might think she was crazy, but thank God he'd finally let her go before she fainted. She didn't know how much more of that man she could take.

Carmel couldn't sleep. She gave up, turned on her lamp and grabbed a magazine from her bedside table. As she flipped through the magazine, she paused at a photo of the supermodel Tyra Banks in lingerie. She stared at Tyra for a long while and sighed. Throwing back the covers, she moved to her mirrored closet doors. She pulled her nightgown over her head and let it drop to the floor.

Carmel cocked her head as she surveyed her body, turning one way, then another. Then she gave a snort of dissatisfaction. She was no Tyra Banks—that was for sure. Fat, she was fat, no way around it. Her breasts were nicely shaped but way too full. Flat was not a word to describe her stomach. And her hips . . . hopeless.

Turning all the way around, she craned her neck to get a good look at her backside. Goodness, it brought to mind a word she learned in high school that had enchanted her at the time. What was it? The word meant the way some African women stored fat in their rear ends. She remembered the picture of the brown woman with enormous buttocks that the word described. *Steatopygia,* that was the word. Her picture could nicely update the one she remembered from high school.

Her thighs were pillows, all soft and billowy. A chocolate Pillsbury dough girl, yep, that described her. She wasn't going to keep any man awake at night wanting this body.

And for some reason, for the first time in her life, that inescapable fact caused her grief. Carmel closed her eyes and shut out her reflection. Those images that were becoming familiar moved across her mind. Steve taking her in his arms, Steve's lips coming down on hers, Steve carrying her to his bed, desire in his eyes . . . His groan as his back gave way from her weight and the thud of her body hitting the floor.

Her eyes snapped open and a mental sound like a record scratching echoed over her dreams. Carmel bit her lip and ran her hand over the soft curve of her stomach, the fleshy width of her hip. No, she was no Tyra Banks, but that didn't mean that she couldn't ever be.

If she were small, she'd match her looks against the best. Everybody always talked about what a pretty face she had. With a body to match, maybe . . . She didn't finish the thought.

She'd always done whatever she really wanted to do. Why should this be any different? She could lose weight if she wanted to. Carmel closed her eyes and pictured Steve's face . . . and the Lord only knew how much she wanted to.

Marvin set the phone in its cradle a little too firmly. "That woman's coming over again. Donna gets like this when Steve won't do what she wants. Starts hovering and coming over here all the time so she can drive both of us nuts."

Carmel didn't look up from the low-fat cookbook she was looking over. She knew a reply wasn't necessary, but she felt the same way. Steve's mother made her uncomfortable. It was the way Donna looked at her, or more exactly, didn't look at her. Her eyes slid past Carmel as if they were afraid to rest on her, as if she was a handicapped person it would be impolite to stare at.

"And what was that stuff you made for lunch?"

Carmel looked up at Marvin's querulous inquiry. "Why? You didn't like it?"

"It was edible, but I miss all that good cooking you used to do. Why are you cooking all these salads with nasty dressing and broiled meat, and no more cherry pies, carrot cake or cinnamon rolls? You trying to put me on some kind of diet?"

Carmel snapped the book shut. "No, Marvin. I'm on a diet."

"Humph. So remember you're the one who needs to be on a diet, not me. I want some real food."

"Thank you for your support," she said, a sarcastic tinge to her voice.

Marvin looked slightly shamefaced. "I don't like diet food, that's all. I like the food you used to cook. Tell you what, if you go back to cooking the old way, I won't let you eat anything fattening."

"You think you can stop me from eating whatever I want?" Carmel sighed. "I'll go back to cooking the way I used to. I was trying to make it a little easier on myself, at least at the start. This dieting is difficult."

Marvin reached out and grasped her shoulder. "I know it's hard, but it's worth it. You go ahead and take off that lard. You'll be a better person and your entire life will improve. I guarantee it."

Carmel's smile belied how she felt inside. Marvin implied that simply because she was fat her life needed improvement, and worse, that she wasn't a good person merely because of her weight. She didn't bother to correct Marvin because she realized that was how a lot of people felt. They believed that being overweight implied a lack of character and a miserable life. It wasn't true. Her character was better than some slim women she knew, and her life was just fine. There was only one little area that needed fine-tuning and that area had to do with men, specifically Steve Reynolds.

"Thanks again for covering for me. I promise I'll be in by nine."

A touch of anger flared through Carmel at Elaine's words. Elaine had been calling in and coming in late frequently, and it was growing into a major problem. "I need to talk to you about your time when you come in," she said.

Silence. "I told you before that I was going through some things."

"I understand. But you're putting me and the other nurses on this case through some things also. I have a family, and I'm going to have to stay over for six hours."

"Why don't you get somebody else to come in? Maybe Lenore would come in early."

"Lenore has put in almost twelve hours overtime this week because of your absences. Not only has she told me she couldn't work any more extra this week, we have to pay her overtime for those hours."

"That's not my problem," Elaine said.

That was the wrong thing to say to Carmel on the third day of her diet.

"Yes, it is. At your next unexcused absence, unemployment is going to be your problem."

What Elaine screamed in her ear was not only rude but downright vulgar. And she had the nerve to slam down the receiver on top of it.

Carmel slowly put the phone back in the cradle. It looked as if she had a major job vacancy to fill. The work had gotten so scarce for RNs at the agency that the ones she usually used were working on cases with other agencies. She'd have to run an ad. Until she hired somebody, she'd have to cope with covering the shifts. Damn. She hated working here in the evening.

You don't want to spend time around Steve until you've lost the weight. She hated to admit it to herself, but the main thing keeping her going was fantasizing about the look in Steve's eyes once he saw her slim and trim. She needed to lose at least sixty-five pounds and here it was day three and she was dying. There was so much food in that damn kitchen, and it was calling her. She'd promised Marvin to cook something good, and she knew to him that meant something rich and fattening. She'd also promised she'd bake him something. It was enough to make a woman want to cuss.

Chapter 8

"Come on out of that kitchen, and come join us at the table like you're civilized," she heard Marvin call from the living room. "Carmel!" he rapped when she didn't reply immediately.

"I'll be in there in a second," she called out. Double damn, she thought. She was trying to get away clean with eating in the kitchen, and Marvin wouldn't even give her that much peace. Steve and his mother were in the dining room and she simply didn't feel up to dealing with them.

She stared at her unsatisfying piece of baked chicken, dry baked potato and the stalks of similarly dry, gray-green, overly crisp broccoli. Then she looked over at the fried chicken, mashed potatoes and gravy, and buttered broccoli on the stove.

Carmel suddenly got up and dumped her food in the trash and heaped her plate with the food from the stove. Screw it. She was hungry, she was stressed. She deserved a good meal. Walking to the dining table, she sat down and defiantly met Marvin's widening eyes when he saw what was on her plate.

He kept his mouth shut for a change, but looked away, his mouth tightening. Donna stared at Carmel's plate. With a faint look of revulsion, her gaze flickered up to Carmel's face, and then she also looked away.

"It's good to see you. I'd almost given up on running into you again," Steve said, pleasure in his eyes. Carmel noticed he never looked once at her plate.

"It's nice to see you again, too. I'll probably be seeing more of you." She directed her attention to Marvin. "Elaine is no longer working for us."

"Thank God," was his only comment.

"I'll have to cover many of her shifts until we find someone else."

Marvin brightened. "That's good. Why do you need to find someone else? I don't believe you couldn't use the money and Lord knows none of you nurses do any work."

"You think hanging out with you isn't work?"

Marvin grinned. "Beats chucking bedpans at the hospital."

Carmel couldn't argue with that. "I need to see my children sometimes," she said.

"Bring them over here," Marvin said.

Donna looked appalled.

"No, I can't do that. But thanks for the offer."

Carmel bit into the chicken leg. It was perfect. The crust was rich, flaky, with melt-in-your-mouth flavor. She followed it with a bite of the potatoes she'd mashed and mixed with cream, butter and salt. Pure pleasure. She relaxed at the table for the first time in days.

"I hoped I'd run into you soon, because I've been wanting to ask you something," Steve said to her.

She smiled at him. Fortified with fried chicken and mashed potatoes, she could handle almost anything.

"I've got tickets to the World Series game tomorrow. Want to go?"

At Steve's question, all thought fled Carmel's mind, along with the apparent power of speech.

Donna choked on the iced tea she'd pointedly poured Sweet 'N Low into a moment before. "How did you get tickets to that game?" she croaked, trying to recover.

Carmel realized with some resentment that Donna's unvoiced question was why was he asking *Carmel* to use one of those prized tickets.

Steve ignored Donna's question and watched her, waiting for her answer. Carmel picked up her napkin and dabbed at her mouth, stalling until she regained her power of speech. "I'd love to go," she managed to finally say.

Steve grinned at her. "That's what I wanted to hear. I'll pick you up at six tomorrow, so we'll have plenty of time to get settled in."

Carmel nodded, too nervous to feel elated. She darted a look at Donna, whose face had whitened and lips were tight. Why was Steve's mother so concerned with whom he asked out? Marvin's eyebrows had shot up so high, she hoped they didn't permanently affix themselves to his hairline.

"Who'd like a piece of apple pie?" Carmel asked.

As Carmel loaded the dishwasher after their meal, her heart sank as Donna swept into the kitchen. Donna wasted no time in getting to the point. "My son does a lot of charity work. He especially has a weak spot for fatherless boys. I had no idea he was taking on heavy women as his next cause."

Daaang, Carmel thought. The witch was tripping. But it was Steve's mother and this was Steve's house. She silently rinsed another plate and put it in the dishwasher.

"You do realize there is no way he could be interested in you, do you? He was telling me the other day how sorry he felt for you," Donna said.

At those last words Carmel's hand trembled a little as she steadily loaded the glasses in the dishwasher.

"You are aware of the caliber of women he dates? Of the woman he married?" Donna continued. "Now don't get me wrong, I'm not merely being mean, I simply don't want you to get your hopes up and be hurt."

Carmel cleared her throat before speaking. "Ms. Reynolds," she started to say.

"Mrs. Graham. My name is Mrs. Graham."

"Mrs. Graham," Carmel continued. "I appreciate your concern. But I'd also appreciate you staying out of my personal business. I'm employed in your son's house and it really isn't appropriate."

Donna's light tan face flushed slightly, and her eyes narrowed. "Anything that concerns my son is my business."

The silence stretched taut between them. Donna spoke first, her voice becoming shrill. "Is it appropriate for you to go out with your employer? I think not. You'd best reconsider his charitable offer."

The woman was out of her mind. Carmel seethed, and it was a minute before she trusted herself to speak. "Excuse me, Mrs. Graham. I have work to do," she said.

She firmly turned her back on Donna, and after a moment she heard the woman leave the kitchen. Carmel felt herself shaking in anger. Steve's mother was a female dog, but the very worst part of it was that she was probably right. She could be nothing but a charity case to Dr. Steve Reynolds. But Carmel would be damned if she'd turn down going to a World Series game with a man that attracted her more than any other man ever had.

Excitement flooded Carmel as her cheers mixed with the roars of the crowd in the stadium. Tom Glavine had struck the batter out. Silence fell as the next batter stepped up and Tom stood on the pitcher's mound. The huge television monitors around the stadium showed beads of sweat gathering on his brow.

She bit her lip. It was a classic scenario, with the bases loaded in the ninth inning and the Braves one run up. Tom Glavine had pitched the entire game with an injured shoulder. Palpable tension along with silent prayers filled the stadium. Could he finish the game? Would Cox pull him out? The bullpen was off while Tom Glavine was on, injured shoulder or no, and now the game rode on him.

"Strrrike one." The crowd roared again and Carmel's tension notched an inch up. One strike, two to go. A walk would tie the game, a significant hit would put the Braves down.

Glavine checked the runners and delivered the ball to the plate. The batter swung.

"Strrrike two."

A wave of excitement swept through the fans as they stood in anticipation of strike three. They hoped. Tom stood on the mound and watched for the signal. A silent mantra echoed through the stadium, *one more time, one more time.* Carmel held her breath as anticipation and anxiety streamed through the air like ribbons.

Suddenly he twirled and threw the ball like a light-ning bolt to the second baseman. "Safe," the umpire cried. The runner stood and brushed himself off.

Glavine turned to face the batter, and the ball flew. The batter swung. Slow motion effect. Carmel closed her eyes as she heard the crack of the bat against the ball.

"It was a foul," Steve yelled over the roar of the crowd.

She chewed a fingernail. Glavine paced the mound, took off his cap and ran his fingers through his hair. Renewed tension built to unbearable heights, and Carmel closed her eyes again. Maybe this was why she never got into sports or horror movies. If something was going to give her a heart attack from anxiety, she didn't want to have paid to get in to see it.

"Strrrike three and he's out!"

The frenzied crowd screamed and Steve whooped and hugged her. "Great game," he shouted.

Carmel smiled weakly. Yeah, it would be, she thought as soon as she recovered from the anxiety of wondering whether Tom would strike the batter out or not.

By the time they reached the car, her adrenaline rush had faded to a glow. She realized that she'd really enjoyed herself. Maybe this sports stuff wasn't so bad after all.

Chapter 9

"That was a game of a lifetime. I really appreciate you bringing me," Carmel said and meant it.

He grinned at her. "Consider it a bonus. You've been so great with Dad. When I first decided to use nurses, since I know my father, I had visions of going through every nursing agency in town. You don't know how much it means to me not to have to."

"I'm glad you didn't have to change agencies. We need the business," Carmel replied. Her voice was steady, but her heart dropped. She'd thought their outing was a date. A few words from him changed it to a favor, a gratuity. *An act of charity?*

They joined the line of cars that crawled toward the stadium parking lot's exit at a snail's pace. "I can tell nobody left this game early. I'm hungry, by the time we get out of this traffic, I'll be starving. Where do you want to eat for a late dinner?"

Eating implied food. At the present moment food implied . . . misery and defeat. Carmel had climbed back into her diet wagon with difficulty, and was fighting to stay on it. The diet wagon was mighty cramped and uncomfortable, and food was the enemy.

"Somewhere I can get a salad or something light. I'm on a diet."

Carmel looked sideways at him from under her lashes to gauge his reaction.

"Well, okay. You make the call. Although if it takes too long to get out of this mess, I might end up using the cell phone to call for a pizza."

"Lord, no!" The exclamation fell involuntarily from Carmel's lips.

Steve looked appalled. "You don't like pizza? I thought everybody liked pizza as long as it didn't have something funky on top like anchovies or pineapple."

"I like pizza. No, let me restate that. I love pizza. That's the problem."

Now he looked puzzled.

"There is no way I could stay on my diet stuck in a car with a pizza. I've only got so much will power," she almost wailed.

Steve cocked his head and stared at her. "Diets are forever, pizza lasts but a moment," he said.

Silence fell at this profound statement.

Carmel drew a breath. "I'm really trying hard to stay on this diet. It's very important to me that I lose weight."

Steve shrugged. "I think diets are overrated. You look fine."

"I guess so," she murmured and stared out the window. Now this hurts, she thought. He doesn't care whether I lose weight or not. He must not see that I have the potential to be just as attractive as the women he dates. I was a fool to hope . . . to hope that maybe he could see through all this lard.

The mood changed and the silence lingered,

slightly uneasy. Steve turned up the jazz station and appeared to get into the mellow saxophone moaning the blues.

The blues fit Carmel's mood. She would have to show Steve Reynolds that she was capable of becoming a desirable, attractive woman. She redoubled her determination to stick to her diet. One day she wouldn't be a charity date to him.

They finally got out of the tangle of cars leaving the stadium. "Umm, Steve? I don't think I want to eat. I don't live too far, could you drop me off?"

He glanced down at her. Was that disappointment in his eyes? No, couldn't be.

When they got to her place, he pulled up to the curb, and Carmel started to get out of the car. She stopped when she saw that Steve had already gotten out of his seat and was on the way to open her door. He helped her out of the seat and followed her as she walked to her door. He'd said he was hungry. Should she ask him in and offer him something to eat? She turned to face him, and pulled up short. Nobody had turned the porch light on. It was dark and he was standing far too close.

"I had a really good time," he said. "Thanks for coming to the game with me."

She looked up him, suddenly losing her breath. "The game was wonderful. I never realized that baseball could be so exciting."

He gave a little crooked smile that made her heart hop. Then he started to bend his head, his lips moving toward her. Carmel felt her body instinctively sway toward him, her eyelids start to close. *You do realize there is no way he could be interested in you, do you? He was telling me the other day how sorry he felt for you,* she heard Donna's voice echo in her head.

Her eyes snapped open. She might have consented

to the charity date, but charity kisses were another matter. Carmel groped behind her for the doorknob. Thank God the door was open. "Thanks again for taking me to the game. I'll see you Monday." And she fled into the house.

Jasmine rolled her eyes yet another time. "Girl, you are tripping so hard I'm surprised you can stand up. What has gotten into you? Moaning and groaning how you aren't good enough for that man."

"I'm fat, Jasmine."

"So? You never used to worry about that. You used to know that the words fat and fine could go together."

Carmel sighed. It was true it was the first time she ever verbalized how she felt. She'd thought she'd ignored society's message about big women. Apparently not. The negative message had seeped into her subconscious, waiting to emerge with her attraction to Steve Reynolds. Ready to torment her with the knowledge that the women Steve had been with were all slim. Suddenly slim meant better.

She hated it. But she couldn't escape her body.

"How would you know?" she said to Jasmine. "You've never been heavy. How many men have been in your life since we decided to start the business together? How many dates have I been on?"

Jasmine's lips tightened, but she said nothing.

"None, Jasmine. No dates, no man. This fat and fine woman as you call me has been batting zero for a long time. I'm twenty-eight years old. Do you think I want to be sitting on the bench watching everybody else play while time goes by and I get older? Don't you think I want what you have?"

Carmel felt tears well in her eyes and prayed they wouldn't spill over to her cheeks.

Jasmine sighed and shook her head. "No, I've never been big. And I'm not saying there isn't a lot of discrimination out there against big people, not to mention the preferences many men have. But that's all they are, preferences. Men like different things, and women come in all flavors."

"And I've never been the flavor of the month," Carmel said, a tinge of bitterness to her voice.

"I think this man, Steve, has caused you to lose all perspective. There is only one reason you have no man in your life: you haven't wanted one. If you did, you'd find a fit that's right for who you are, instead of trying to mold yourself to squeeze into something too tight. There is somebody, no there are multiple somebodies, out there who will appreciate who you are. You're trying on the wrong outfit."

"But it's the outfit I want to wear," Carmel whispered.

Jasmine shook her head again. "Girl, I don't know what to do with you. But this is the first time since I've known you that you've tripped over a man, so I guess you're entitled. Lord knows I've lost my mind over some man a time or two."

"What makes you think you ever got it back?"

Jasmine grinned. "Now that's the Carmel I know and love. I'm starving. Want to take the kids out to eat? They've been complaining about the low-fat dinners."

"Sure," Carmel said, feeling desperate and grim. Jasmine was truly fortunate she'd never understand how it felt to be hungry and know that food was the enemy.

* * *

Steve pulled away from Carmel's house feeling somewhat off balance. The look in her eyes when he'd started to kiss her had looked more like consternation than passionate longing. He hadn't considered the possibility that she might not be attracted to him. She might even be interested in another man.

Maybe he'd pushed her too hard. She worked in his house, and technically she was his employee. A sexual overture by any definition could be termed harassment. Dismay filled him. Was it obligation that caused her to accompany him to the game?

But the pull between them when they were together was undeniable. It was as if they both were magnetized, and the attraction had to come from her as much as from him. Possibly ambivalence was her conflict. Since she was employed in his home, ambivalence to his overtures would be a natural response. He needed to back off and give her time and space.

The situation wouldn't last forever. He'd come to the conclusion that physical therapy would probably assist his father more than the nurses, but surprisingly his father was adamant about keeping the nurses on. Dad had quickly become accustomed to having women waiting on him hand and foot twenty-four seven. That was fine with him. He liked having Carmel around.

He'd try another approach. Friendship was a sound basis of any relationship, and friendship with Carmel would be a fine foundation to build on.

"Dinner's ready," Carmel heard Joy, the housekeeper-cum-cook, call from downstairs.

She sat on the floor in Marvin's room amidst piles

of paper. He'd decided they would tackle the project of sorting and organizing his files this evening.

"Just leave that stuff there, we'll finish it after we eat," Marvin said, trying and failing to heave himself out of the recliner he'd enthroned himself in to supervise Carmel.

"Wait for me to help you. I don't want you falling again."

She helped Marvin down the stairs and followed the odor of delicious food wafting from the dining room. She almost groaned when she saw Donna standing at the foot of the stairs, tapping her foot impatiently.

"I take it my son's not home yet?" she asked Marvin.

He ignored her words and walked past her toward the dining room.

"Marvin! I was talking to you."

He looked at Carmel, a gleam in his eye. "I thought I heard something. Did you hear something?"

Carmel suppressed a smile, and said nothing.

"I'm not in the mood to play games, Marvin," Donna said, following them.

"They sound like a bee buzzing in the clover, folks coming into my house asking questions and making demands without the decency to speak first."

Donna frowned. "Damn you, Marvin," she muttered. They'd reached the dining room, and Carmel's stomach growled at the sight of the food. Looked like they were having pot roast tonight.

"Joy, set a place for me. I'm staying for dinner," Donna called into the kitchen.

"Some folks have the decency at least to ask the people who live in a house if they can stay for dinner," Marvin observed.

Donna rolled her eyes. "Please, Marvin. You're starting to get on my last nerve."

"Like you aren't always sitting on mine? Don't you ever spend any time at your own home anymore? What's that husband of yours doing for dinner?"

"Gene is working."

"Ahhhh," Marvin said, a wealth of meaning in that syllable.

Joy bustled in with another place setting for Donna. They settled at the table and Carmel noted with dismay that there was no plate where she customarily sat. She'd pushed back her chair to go to the kitchen when Joy came out with a steaming plate of food.

"I thought I'd cook a better dinner for you since you told me how important your diet was to you," Joy said, setting the plate down in front of Carmel with a flourish.

"Thank you, it looks wonderful," Carmel said, trying to inject the right note of gratitude in her voice. The broiled chicken breast and half a baked potato without butter or sour cream looked mighty unappetizing compared to the savory pot roast with carrots, new potatoes and onions heaped beside it. The string beans on her plate looked like grass compared to the sweet peas with a generous pat of real butter melting among them.

"Here you are, Carmel, I almost forgot." Joy proffered a generous green salad and a bottle of fat-free ranch dressing. Carmel hated those fat-free dressings. No matter how much she tried, she couldn't acquire a taste for them. She didn't care for plain vinegar or lemon juices either, so she'd been forgoing salads altogether.

Marvin beamed as he surveyed her plate. "You're doing mighty fine there. Keep up the good work, and you'll be slim and trim in no time."

"With as much weight as Carmel has to lose, I doubt if it will take no time. But if she can manage to exercise a little self-discipline the weight will eventually come off,'' Donna said.

Before Carmel could tell her to mind her own business, Donna added, ''By the way, how was the game last weekend? I heard you accompanied my son after all.''

''The game was great.'' Carmel picked up her knife and fork and concentrated pointedly on her food.

''So why are you showing up here for dinner again?'' Marvin asked Donna.

''My son didn't return my call when I paged him. I need to talk to him.''

At that moment Steve walked into the dining room, looking so good that Carmel almost choked on a green bean.

''Hi, Mom, Dad. It's good to see you here in the evening again, Carmel.''

He sat down and helped himself to a generous portion of pot roast.

''Carmel tells me she enjoyed your little outing last weekend,'' Donna said. ''It was so *charitable* for you to take her out like that. I'm sure she's very grateful.''

''Charity had nothing to do with it, Mom,'' Steve said. Carmel's heart rose, and fell just as quickly when he added, ''Carmel has worked very hard here, and I'm extremely pleased with her work. The situation with the nurses couldn't have worked out better. Frankly, knowing how you are, Dad, I was worried. I'm grateful to Carmel for taking one more worry off my mind.''

Gratitude was almost as bad as charity. She'd been right when she concluded there was no way Dr. Steve Reynolds could be attracted to her, to want to spend time in her company and get to know her better. He was clear as a bell. The game had been nothing more than a generous tip for her nursing services.

Suddenly, Carmel felt sick. She wanted to push back her plate of low-calorie, low-fat food and leave the table to nurse her pain.

"Isn't that nice," Donna said. "And so generous of you when there was so many other women who would be happy to have gone to the game with you." She turned to Carmel. "Were you comfortable, dear? Those chairs at the stadium are so small."

"Quite comfortable, thank you," she replied, longing to slap the smirk off Donna's face. Why in God's name was the woman so hostile?

"I've been paging you all day. Why didn't you return my call?" Donna asked.

"I've been busy. The switchboard operator marked none of the calls urgent."

"So that's why she asks if it's a family emergency. Next time I'll know what to say to get you to call me back."

"If I call back on an urgent message, and it's short of death or disaster, I'm not going to be too happy."

Donna sniffed. "Anyway, I need to talk to you after dinner privately.

"At least you're going to have the decency to let the man eat in peace for once," Marvin said. "And apologize to Carmel for that crack about the stadium chairs. I won't have you being rude to her."

Donna stared at Marvin. "Rude? You have the gall to call someone else rude?"

Before Marvin could answer, Steve laid his fork on his plate with a clatter. "It's been a tough day at work, and I'm tired of coming home to all this bickering. You know you're welcome in my home at any time, Mom, but if you and Dad can't manage a pleasant atmosphere at the dinner table, I'm taking my meals elsewhere."

Silence. Steve picked his fork back up. "How was your day, Dad?"

"Pretty good. Carmel is helping me get those file cabinets cleaned out. You know I've been wanting to do that for years."

The conversation settled into banal small talk, but none of Carmel's tension eased. She cleaned her plate and excused herself. When she entered the kitchen, Joy was taking a bundt cake out of the oven and Carmel's mouth watered. "You're done eating already? Here, I have an apple for you."

"No thanks. I have some things to do upstairs." Carmel placed her dish in the sink and cast a longing gaze at the cake before she fled upstairs.

Chapter 10

After dinner, she sorted Marvin's papers. She was about to call it a night when she heard a tap on the door. "Come on in," she called, wondering whether she should file some of the papers or leave them for Marvin to look through. She wondered why Marvin would bother to knock. Maybe he thought she was still upset.

"Carmel." Her head shot up at the sound of Steve's voice. She struggled to her feet, ignoring his proffered hand of assistance.

"Yes?" Carmel smoothed the front of her white slacks.

"I wanted to talk to you." He cleared his throat and paused. "I wanted to let you know how much I enjoyed your company at the game."

"I had a good time, too."

"Mainly, I wanted to make sure you didn't feel obligated by the invitation or misunderstand in any way. I wanted you to come because I'm so pleased with how Dad is doing."

Carmel looked away, the words painful. When she looked back, her gaze was resolute. "Your dad doesn't really need nurses, you know. RNs are especially superfluous. A physical therapist would be better to help with his weakness and occasional lack of balance."

"I've come to the same conclusion myself. Dad likes the nurses though, especially you, and he can afford the luxury. I'll let him call the shots. But a physical therapist is coming out tomorrow. They'll be doing home visits."

"I'm surprised Marvin didn't say anything to me about it."

"Well, that's probably because he doesn't know yet. That was my second topic to discuss. Could you be sure and be present during the visit? Sort of to smooth things over?"

Carmel's lips tightened. "I don't think so. Your dad doesn't take too well to having things sprung on him. Since this is something you sprang, I think you'd better handle it."

Steve's eyebrows shot up and Carmel sunk to the floor again and picked up a piece of paper. "Excuse me. I really need to get these papers filed before I go home this evening."

After Steve left, she bit her lips in a visible effort to pull herself together. So she was a little crabby to him. He deserved it. He came in here to explain why he took her to the game, so she wouldn't embarrass him with some crush, or mess up his fancy suits drooling over him. Well, hell would proverbially freeze over before she ever let him know . . . ever let him know how much she wanted him . . .

* * *

It was 9:30 when Carmel got home. The house was dark, but she heard the TV from the family room. She missed her evenings with the kids and the long heart-to-hearts with Jasmine.

She went into the kitchen, opened the refrigerator and stared at the leftover macaroni and cheese and fried catfish her mother must have made for dinner tonight. Leftover creamy rice pudding. Sandwich fixings. Ice cream. Tears ran down her face, silent and unexpected. Carmel resolutely turned away from the refrigerator to the counter and wiped her face with a paper towel.

She gasped a few deep breaths because the pain felt as if a stranger had made a quick one-two punch in her gut, then inexplicably darted away. What was wrong with her? She was falling apart ... Her thoughts disintegrated into need, and she made a quick movement. The bowl of rice pudding and a spoon were in her hands and she bolted for the sanctuary of her room.

She locked her door behind her and sat down cross-legged in the middle of her bed. She wiped her eyes and shook her head, but she didn't think, didn't stop her hand from moving to her mouth in a quick and methodical fashion.

Fifteen minutes later, the bowl of rice pudding nothing but a memory, Carmel fell back on the bed, calmed by the infusion of sugar, butter and real cream. There had probably been about six cups of pudding in that bowl, now scraped clean.

She felt uncomfortable and nauseated from the too-large amount of rich food eaten way too quickly. She felt like she should cry, not from the dregs of emotion that threatened to bubble up before she stuffed down the rice pudding, but because of the diet smashed into smithereens and lying crushed in the empty bowl of rice pudding.

She was a gluttonous fat pig and she'd always be a gluttonous fat pig. Who was she to hope for a life like slim women had the possibility of having? A life where a man cherishes you and loves you, where you feel beautiful, sexy and desirable?

She was entitled to none of these things. She had it okay, great kids, a skill and profession that would allow her to maintain their fairly comfortable lifestyle. She wasn't running the streets, nor chasing after any man. She didn't drink too much or blow her paycheck running up to Atlantic City to play the casinos on long weekends.

She had family, and a few friends, people who cared about her. She had quite a bit, more than a lot of other women. She had no right to feel miserable and sorry for herself. There were plenty of heavy women in Atlanta, and she wondered how many of them were stifling their lonely tears in a bowl of comfort food.

She wondered how many of them locked themselves in their bedrooms and ate until they wanted to throw up. Probably only her, pathetic fat pig Carmel Matthews.

She heard a tap on the door. She took a deep breath, grabbed the bowl and stuffed it under her bed. She ran her hand hurriedly over her face to wipe away errant traces of rice pudding and called out in a firm voice, "Come in."

The doorknob shook. "The door's locked," her mother called. Carmel quickly got up to unlock it and her mother pushed right past her into the room, her eyes searching.

Irritation worked its way around the rice pudding in Carmel's belly. Now was not the time that she had the slightest desire to listen to her mother about . . . anything really.

"I thought I heard you come in," Mama said. "The kids don't know you're here yet. Why didn't you say something when you got in? That's not like you."

"It's been a hard day. I needed to relax on my own awhile."

"What's been going on with you? What's wrong? Melanie came to me today complaining about how grouchy you are since you've been dieting. That's not like you either."

"I'm trying to lose some weight."

"And driving everybody else, not to mention yourself, crazy in the process."

"Mama, I've got to lose this weight."

"You don't got to do anything but stay black and die. Every single one of the women in your family, on both sides, are heavy."

"So you're saying I should just forget it and live my life out as fat as a pig because of genetics?"

"What I'm saying is that you are probably going to be heavy no matter what you do," Mama said. "After your aunt Mary was diagnosed with diabetes, she cut out the sugar and exercised. She doesn't have to take any medication anymore, and her doctor says as long as she keeps everything up she doesn't have to worry about diabetes anymore."

"Aunt Mary still weighs well over two hundred pounds."

"That's my point. Your aunt Mary is healthier, says she feels better than she ever has in her life. But she didn't lose hardly an ounce of weight. Although she says she dropped a few clothing sizes replacing all that fat with muscle, she's still big." Her mother sat on the edge of the bed. Carmel stayed standing by the door, her arms crossed over her chest. She wished her mother would leave. She couldn't think of any topic she wanted to discuss less at this moment.

Mama continued. "I've seen what you're going through happen too many times with my own sisters, your cousins. Going on a diet to look like one of them women in the magazines or on TV. It just makes us folks bigger and more evil. Diets don't work with our type of people. If there ain't no famine going on, there is no way we are going to look like one of them skinny, starved-looking women them white men think is so fine."

"Not only white men," Carmel muttered.

Her mom gave her a sharp look.

"I have to lose weight. I'll be thirty in no time and look at me. I don't have a life."

"Losing weight isn't going to fix that."

"At this rate I guess not. I don't seem to get through a day without going crazy on food and messing up."

"That's what I'm saying. Baby, you can get tighter, you can get in good shape. But the odds of you getting into a size eight are pretty skinny. And there are plenty of size eights out there who have way more problems than you do."

Carmel shrugged, still unmoved, and her mother sighed. "Have you seen what's happening to your daughter with this diet mess? You've been working long hours these past couple of weeks."

"No. What's going on?" Carmel unfolded her arms and moved to her upholstered chair in the corner. She leaned toward her mother, concerned.

"She's got this idea in her head that she's fat and ugly. She says she's on a diet. I couldn't imagine that you'd put your daughter on the type of diet she says she's on."

A sinking feeling dropped into Carmel's stomach.

"I had no idea. She's not fat, just solid and athletic. What diet does she say she's on?"

"Some crazy thing where you eat only meat. She won't even eat vegetables and fruits. It can't be good for her."

"Damn. I'll have to talk to her."

"Like mother, like daughter. You need to talk some sense into yourself first. Why don't you stop trying to starve yourself and eat some good food? Things haven't changed since my grandmother said to get some fresh air and exercise and cut down on the starch, the grease and the sugar. That's all you need to do. All these fancy diets those folks make up is a bunch of crap made up to waste your money."

Her mother stood. "There's not a thing wrong with getting healthy," she repeated. "But Melanie has the same type of body everyone else in the family has. We're not meant to be small. And you need to get it through your head and then your daughter's that you don't need to be a little bitty thing to get a man. Most men like the feel of a woman and all the curves that go with them. They don't want all bones and muscle, and the ones who think they do are brainwashed. Seems like the more women look like men to those fashion folks, the better. Shoot, if those fashion designers said that women with facial hair were in style, some women would be crazy enough to try to get a beard, and some men would be crazy enough to want them."

Mama moved to the door. "What you need to do is to lay off all those sweets you eat when you're bothered." She glanced around the room again. "And don't leave empty dishes in your room. You'll attract bugs." With those words, she swept her three-hundred-pound body gracefully out of the room.

Carmel stared after her. Her mother might have a

point, but she wasn't ready to give up the hope of reaching the accepted standard of beauty. She'd seen a picture of Steve's ex-wife Sienna in *Jet* magazine the other day at some charity function. The woman looked beautiful.

No way would Sienna Lake have been considered beautiful at Carmel's weight. The chance was slim Sienna would have made it in the corporate world if she didn't look the way she did. An envious voice whispered in Carmel's head that men did the promoting, didn't they? Even if Sienna had become successful, if she were also fat, there would always be that one thing, that one area where she didn't quite measure up.

For once, Carmel wanted to feel like Sienna must have felt when that picture was snapped. To preen for the camera instead of wince and wish you could hide. No, even if her mother had a point, she wasn't ready to give up the dream yet. She had to do it. She had to lose weight.

Chapter 11

Later that night, Carmel sat up against her headboard, staring unseeingly at the book propped up on her knees. Her daughter Melanie was hurting. With a mother's perception, tonight she saw the newly bruised look in her daughter's eyes. What pained Carmel was that she hadn't even been aware of what was going on with her daughter. Her mother had seen it first.

Something would have to change. She couldn't go on working these long hours. She'd talk to Marvin and Steve about doing away with night shift and move Lenore to evenings. Marvin could do without somebody watching him sleep, and while the agency could certainly use the income, she was going to have to let the money go.

The thought that she wouldn't see Steve nearly so often was bittersweet. She had no use for his gratitude, and the thought that he wasn't attracted to her was painful. But being in his presence was sweet. At heart, he was such a nice man. Intelligent, gentle, but she sensed an edge to him that added up to that touch of interest that could make a man so exciting. Yes, Dr. Steve Reynolds was all that and more.

Marvin grumbled but agreed the night nurses weren't necessary. Lenore said she'd be happy to switch to evenings. So far, so good, Carmel thought. But she'd left the hardest part for last. Hesitating before the door to Steve's office, she took a deep breath before she knocked.

"Come in," he called. He was sitting at his desk, a medical journal in his hand. He met her eyes and smiled, and Carmel swallowed hard. Damn the man for being so fine.

"I need to cut my hours," Carmel said in a rush.

Steve frowned.

"I need to spend more time with my kids. Trey says he misses me at home in the evenings hounding him about his homework, and Melanie's at that age where . . . well, I worry about her."

"You're going to have a hard time convincing Dad that another nurse can fill your shoes."

"That's the main thing I want to talk to you about. I haven't been able to find another nurse. Marvin and I agree he doesn't need night nurses to sit there and watch him sleep."

"True." Steve picked up a pencil and tapped it on his desk. "You'll still be here days?"

"I plan to be."

"Good." His eyes twinkled at her. "Your presence at the dinner table will be sorely missed. Sometimes we need a gentle presence to take the edge off all of the, er, controversy."

Carmel agreed silently that something was needed, although she doubted it was she.

He stood up and moved closer to her. "I'm glad you came in. I've been wanting to talk to you."

He hesitated and looked at his hands. He seemed a little uneasy. Carmel couldn't imagine what subject concerning her would make him seem that way.

"Since we went to the game together, especially since what happened after the game, things have been a little strained between us."

Carmel immediately flashed back to the memory of his lips moving closer to hers as they stood on her front steps after the game.

"I don't want you to feel strained or uncomfortable by what I did—was going to do."

Now she looked down. "I don't. I went inside because I didn't want you to feel obligated. I didn't want a charity kiss."

"A charity kiss?"

"You know, like what you do after a date. Kiss goodbye, whether you mean it or not. Although I know taking me to the game wasn't a date. You said it was an act of gratitude."

There was a moment of silence, and he moved closer. "Carmel, charity or gratitude had nothing whatsoever to do with my wanting to be with you."

She looked up at him, startled. "I—" Her eyes caught his, and she lost all thought. The desire that glowed within his eyes turned her brain to pudding.

It wasn't a conscious movement that swayed her body toward his, that tipped her chin up to accept his kiss. He moved toward her too, almost imperceptibly. His hands caressed her arms and pulled her closer. Then his lips touched hers like a whisper.

The kiss deepened, exploring, urgent, quickly turning fevered. Sensations whirled and skidded through Carmel, mixed with a sense of wonder. This couldn't be happening, this man couldn't be holding her in his arms, tight and hard like he meant it. His long, hard body pressed against hers, and his tongue lazily, intimately exploring the recesses of her mouth. A slow, hard burn started somewhere near the pit of her stomach and rapidly worked its way south.

She couldn't stop her body from arching against him. His lips nuzzled her cheek, her neck. A soft sigh of pleasure escaped her lips. His lips touched hers again, and demanded more. His arousal, hard and unmistakable, beckoned a passion she didn't know existed within her.

A tap at the door. Steve's head lifted. They parted, seemingly in slow motion, both breathing hard.

"Steve?" Joy's voice called through the door. "Marvin told me to tell Carmel the physical therapist is here, but I can't find her. He won't let the therapist touch him without her there."

"I'll be out in a moment," Carmel called, her voice surprisingly steady.

Joy's footsteps receded.

"I better go," she said.

"Call me down if you need me."

"All right," she said. She turned to the door.

"Carmel?" She paused and looked back at Steve.

His gaze was serious. "I want to be with you because of your generous spirit, your gentle ways, the way you put Dad in his place, your smile, the love you show for your children. Charity or gratitude has nothing to do with it. Understand?" he asked.

She nodded and slipped out of the room, too bemused to analyze anything further.

* * *

The physical therapist looked like Halle Berry's twin. Although she seemed to be around Carmel's height and age, the therapist probably weighed 110 pounds soaking wet. "Come on, Dr. Reynolds, one more time," she chirped.

Carmel observed Marvin give a token grumble. When he said, "My name is Marvin. There are two Dr. Reynolds in this house," Carmel knew the girl was in with him.

"What's a fine woman like yourself doing having to work?" he asked the physical therapist as she walked backward in front of him, observing his gait.

Behind them, Carmel's lips tightened. So Marvin thought the world of employment was only necessary for fat women like herself who couldn't get a man?

When the woman left after assuring them she was coming three evenings a week, Marvin sank in the chair. "Carmel, if you had a shape on you like that, you'd look just as good as that girl does. If she doesn't give you incentive, I don't know what will. Mmmm-mmmm-mmmm, that girl was fine. Where's my son?"

"He's in his office."

"No matter, he'll meet her soon enough. You better start dropping that weight with fine women like that dropping in."

"It's time for me to go home. I'll be back in the morning like we discussed," Carmel said through stiff lips.

"All right. You remember what I'm telling you, you hear? You stick with that diet."

Carmel couldn't get out of that house fast enough.

* * *

She went to bed early, leaving her mother and children in front of the blare of TV. She felt over-wrought, overloaded as she touched her lips and absorbed the fact of Steve's kiss. He'd wanted her and he'd kissed her with unmistakable passion. He'd said charity or gratitude had nothing to do with it. Her generous spirit, her gentle ways, the way she got along with his dad, her smile, the love she showed for her children were what he stated as her attractions. He'd asked if she understood.

She understood him only too well. He'd mentioned nothing about being attracted to her physically, about thinking she was beautiful, about wanting every inch of her.

Carmel supposed it was a good thing when a man wanted you for your character and personality, but her question was how strong were those things against the pull of physical attraction? She didn't want to be one of those women whom men cheated on, but never actually left. "I love my wife," they'd say. They did their husbandly duty once a week while they were feverishly loving some other woman every stolen moment they could get. Mama told her that had been the deal with her father, although the man never did actually marry her.

She wanted more than that. *Settle for what you can get, fool. It's more than you ever hoped for from a man like that,* the treacherous voice in her head whispered.

The problem was that she'd never been the settling type. If she had been, she'd have some man up in here, sitting in her den, flipping the channels with the remote, and giving her some loving every other night. She'd craved the feel of a man within her. If she would settle, there was always some man who needed a place to stay and some good home cooking. "You're one fine woman. I'd sure like to be with you.'' Keep dreaming, she'd think and not break stride. Nope, she'd never settled into anything except her own loneliness.

Don't screw it up. Don't demand more from Steve than you are worth. Carmel stared at her hands. Her fingers were pudgy and round. She tried to keep them up, though she'd never been one for those long fake nails. She kept them cut short, clean and polished with clear or light polish. She eyed the fleshy roundness of her fingers, her wrists. She never wore rings, not wanting to draw attention to her fat fingers. Never thought her hands were pretty enough for any kind of ring. She buried her face in her hands. She had to lose weight. Her very life depended on it.

Chapter 12

Saturday morning cartoons blared from the den. The transition between sleep and wakefulness had been abrupt, jarring Carmel out of troubling dreams she couldn't quite remember. She blinked up at the ceiling, ticking off mentally what she needed to accomplish today. Laundry, grocery shopping, the house badly needed a good once-over, talk to Melanie.

Talk to Melanie. She'd tried to broach the subject of dieting with her last night when she tried to talk about the necessity of a balanced diet when trying to lose weight.

Melanie had stared at her, uncharacteristically non-forthcoming. "How much weight have you lost, Mom? Don't look like it's been a whole lot."

The question had stunned Carmel into silence. She gave the weak reply that a diet that keeps the weight off takes time, then she changed the subject. She couldn't look into her daughter's face to see the reaction to her words. It would have hurt too much.

She'd have to pick up the conversation today, painful or not. Melanie was growing, and her thirteen-year-old body had started sprouting the trappings of a woman. She'd not have her daughter harming herself. Carmel had made low-fat pasta primavera last night. She'd covered the pasta with a generous amount of vegetables, and she made the dish fragrant with garlic and Parmesan cheese and a touch of olive oil. A tossed salad and warm bread sticks accompanied the meal.

Melanie had ignored the meal and gone to the refrigerator and carved a hunk from the large ham Carmel had cooked for a previous dinner.

Carmel threw the covers off her. No point in delaying the day. Difficult tasks put off never went away, they simply got worse.

When she entered the den, Trey was sprawled over the couch while he nursed a bowl of brightly colored cold cereal. "Hey, Mom," he said, his eyes never leaving the television set.

"Good morning, baby," she replied.

Melanie nodded, but didn't look up. She had what looked like a bowl full of at least a dozen boiled eggs cradled in her lap as she sat on the carpeted floor, a salt shaker at her side.

Carmel's lips tightened. This made no sense. The way the girl was eating had to stop. "Melanie, I want to talk to you. Come with me."

"Mom, not now, I want to watch this show."

"Now."

Melanie heaved herself up off the floor with all the rebellious body language a teenage girl could muster. Carmel turned and walked toward the living room without looking back. She sat on the couch and patted the place beside her as Melanie entered the room.

Her daughter remained standing in the middle of the room, her arms folded across her chest. "You want to talk to me about my diet, don't you?"

"Good guess," Carmel replied. "If you were older, I'd let you see this diet through. But you're only thirteen. Your body is growing and needs the proper nutrients."

Melanie spoke as if she hadn't heard her. "I've lost ten pounds in ten days, Mom. If I stay on this diet, I'll be Alexis's size in a month. It really works."

"That's mostly water loss, honey. It'll come back as soon as you go back to eating a balanced diet—"

"You're just jealous of me because you can't stick to a diet and lose weight," Melanie said, her voice rising.

Carmel's hand itched to slap her. She remained silent for a moment because she realized Melanie's statement hurt because it was so close to home. But that didn't mean she wasn't right about her daughter. It was imperative that she eat a variety of foods.

"Your diet will change as of right now. If you want to lose weight, cut down on your calories and fat and exercise more, but no more unbalanced, crazy diets."

"I'm not going to quit my diet. You can't make me. You're just scared that I'll get a boyfriend. You want me to stay fat and ugly and all alone like you!"

Carmel's eyes narrowed. "Go to your room," she said quietly. Melanie didn't move.

"I'd advise you to get to your room right now while you're still capable of walking there."

Her daughter took one look at her mother's face and exited quickly. Carmel leaned back against the couch, reeling. She felt as if she'd done a couple rounds in a heavyweight title fight. But she knew she'd hardly started the first skirmish. Problem was she had no idea what to do next. Her daughter had lost her tiny little thirteen-year-old mind, but Melanie had a point that she couldn't be forced to eat what she didn't want to.

Her mother would have knocked her out if she'd ever spoken to her like Melanie had just spoken to Carmel. She'd have hit the floor before she ended the first sentence. What was wrong with the kids nowadays? Carmel couldn't shake the feeling it was something wrong with the way she'd brought them up. Those modern ideas of child rearing and discipline had slipped into her consciousness, as they had with most other parents of her generation. She had a feeling that a consensus was growing that the older generation might have been right about the take-no-guff and spare-no-rod school of child rearing.

Below all the worries that Carmel had about Melanie, her words still echoed and rang around in her head. "Fat and ugly and all alone like you." So that was what her daughter thought of her? A pathetic, lonely, unattractive woman no one wanted? God, that hurt. She slowly got up and went back to her room. Time to call in the reinforcements. But the only one she could think to talk to was her mother. Jasmine could never understand.

The doorbell rang before she reached the phone. "Mom, Jasmine's here," she heard Trey call. She wheeled, happy at the prospect of seeing Jasmine and irritated at the same time at having the call to her mother postponed and the time to lick her wounds interrupted.

"I have something to tell you," Jasmine said before Carmel had even gotten back into the living room.

"I can't handle too much more," she replied, sinking back into the couch.

"What's going on?"

"Melanie is giving me fits."

"That's a new one. Your kids hardly ever gave you any trouble before."

"I never had a kid reach thirteen before."

"I heard about some debate in Congress to emancipate them at that age. Especially girls," Jasmine said with a straight face. "Boy trouble already?"

"This feels worse for some reason. Melanie is on a diet."

There was a pause as Jasmine obviously waited for Carmel to continue.

"Is that it?" she finally asked.

"That's enough. She's determined to stick to this crazy diet."

"Carmel, I hate to break this to you, but you've been driving everybody nuts with your diet for a couple of weeks now. What's your trouble about Melanie going on a diet, too?"

"I wouldn't expect you to understand."

"Why not? Although it might help if you got around to telling me what the trouble is."

"One of my troubles is women who should have no problems at all in life coming here and telling me I don't have any troubles."

Jasmine frowned. "No problems at all in life? I know you're not talking about me. So what are you talking about?"

"You've been thin all your life, haven't you? You've never had to deal with anything like what Melanie and I are wrestling with. You've always had it made. Of course you can't understand."

"I don't see why you make such a big deal out of it. Eat less, lose weight. One-two-three, how hard can that be?"

"Why don't you package that formula, sell it and

make a billion dollars?'' Carmel snapped. "Yep, losing weight is easy. I just stay this way because I just love my daughter calling me fat and ugly and trying to starve herself so she won't turn out like me. I get a real kick out of being disgusting and alone. I'm just having the time of my life.''

"Carmel,'' Jasmine started to say.

"Just leave,'' Carmel said, fighting to choke back her tears.

Jasmine started to say something, then closed her mouth. She put her coat back on and turned for the door. "I am your friend. I just run off at the mouth sometimes and I'm sorry.'' Jasmine shook her head. "I'll call you later.'' She shut the door quietly behind her.

Carmel headed back to her room to that quiet space she needed more sorely than ever now. The call to her mother about Melanie would have to wait.

Chapter 13

Steve gazed at her hungrily. He reclined on what looked like puffy white clouds. His chest was muscled and sprinkled with hair. His loins were clad in loose midnight blue silk pajama bottoms and his feet were bare. He looked yummy enough to eat.

Then Carmel saw herself as if slowly coming into focus from a wide-angle lens. She gasped. Was that really her? Decapitate Angela Bassett and stick her own head on top and that would come close to this vision of herself. She had on a frothy white teddy that matched the clouds, with generous honey-colored breasts spilling out of the top.

Those breasts were the only fat present on her rock-hard body with the muscles of an eighteen-year-old boy transplanted to a mature female frame. She was tall, hard and tight and could be a fashion model. She was the epitome of North American beauty.

She saw the bulge of Steve's erection and felt pure feminine pride in the knowledge that the sight of her body was driving him wild. Oh, yeah. She eased the straps of the teddy over *her shoulders and gyrated to the beat of the music that had suddenly started to thump around them. Stripper music. She flexed her bulging biceps in time to the beat, and swayed back and forth.*

She noted Steve's slack mouth, and the bulge in his pants had reached gargantuan proportions, but he wasn't drooling yet. To fix that, she pulled the teddy over her breasts. Her mysteriously firm breasts looked appetizing, but didn't bounce when she moved and felt like rocks. Oh, well. She supposed thin women's breasts were firm like the rest of them.

She exposed her rock-hard belly, with washboard abs visible, and did a little shimmy and grind. Steve quivered in anticipation, and she started to draw the teddy down over her—

She looked down and it was unmistakable. She stared at Steve, feeling utter panic, but he'd started to shrink, becoming impossibly small, his bulge deflating and disappearing first.

Below her belly button, from a thatch of curly hair, erupted strange masculine appendages. Not only had she become the epitome of American beauty, she had become a boy.

The boom, boom, boom of the stripper music thudding louder and louder drowned out her rising shriek of horror.

She woke with a start, the thud of the music still echoing in her ears and matching the pounding of her heart. What a nightmare. Lord have mercy, even her erotic dreams were downers. She willed herself not to peek under the covers to see if she was still intact and unchanged. The dream had been so real. She'd looked like a fashion model, the pinnacle of womanly American beauty. And it turned out she'd been transformed into an eighteen-year-old transvestite boy with fake boobs. It had all looked like the same thing.

Is that what you want to be, girl? Some kind of freak? The voice that echoed in her mind sounded just like her mother.

"You're trying to starve yourself to look like what those fashion folks want you to look like," Mama had said last night on the phone. "Wake up, child. Those folks want you to look like what they lust after, and that looks like young pretty teenage boys to me. Don't no real man want no boy-looking woman less he been brainwashed. I thought I raised you with more sense. Yep, them fashion folks got the American public bamboozled. But nobody ever said that the American public is too bright. Look at that fool they voted up in Congress ..." Then her Mama segued into one of her political rants. Fashion, politics, it was all the same game to Mama.

Carmel threw back the covers and sighed as she made her way to the bathroom. Basically Mama said that she'd need to get herself together before she could help Melanie. It felt like Mama was right. Problem was Carmel had no idea where to begin tackling the issues of body image, cultural attractiveness, sexual desirability and self-acceptance either for herself or her daughter.

Carmel turned on the water in the sink and stared at her face in the mirror. Such a pretty face. How many times had she heard that before? How many times had she resented the words and the implication beneath them? Such an ugly body.

The voices from her past were simply too loud, and the tapes they recorded played over and over.

"I'd rather be dead than fat." The voice of a fellow nursing student, bony and blonde, whispering *sotto voce* to another in the ladies room while she darted a venomous glance over Carmel.

"Damn, baby, you'd be fine if you'd drop a few pounds." The husky whisper from an old flame, her dreams of love and acceptance dissipating with his words.

She couldn't forget all those popular and media images of women accounted beautiful. "You've got such a pretty face . . ."

It used to be the white women who carried the heaviest burden of unrealistic body conformity, but their cultural standards were trickling into the beauty standards of the minority population. The black actresses and models were becoming as muscled and bony as the rest of the women accounted beautiful in their professions.

But while she knew all this intellectually, it had yet to settle into her heart. Carmel wanted to be counted as attractive. She didn't want to carry all the baggage society heaped upon heavy women, she wanted . . . she wanted Steve Reynolds.

She dropped her nightgown to the floor and stood on the scale. The needle settled and Carmel wanted to scream. The dieting wasn't working. When she slipped, she slipped hard. She always climbed back on, but it seemed as if one of her slips made up all the calorie deficits and more. She'd gained half a pound since she started dieting. She thought about weighing well over two hundred pounds for the rest of her life, and she felt something die inside. Closing her eyes to block out the pain, she blindly reached for her nightgown and slipped it back over her head.

"Carmel?" Jasmine's voice sounded unusually tentative over the phone lines. A tinge of guilt tugged at Carmel for going off on her, and she gripped the receiver tightly. Jasmine couldn't help it that she had it made, that life had handed her a gift on a silver platter, that—

"I wanted to apologize for not empathizing with your dieting challenges," Jasmine said.

"It's all right. I shouldn't expect you to."

"Well, it was hell when I quit smoking years ago, but at least I could quit cold turkey. I didn't have to smoke three cigarettes a day."

Carmel sighed heavily. "I'm at wit's end. You know I work hard, and I've always accomplished whatever I've set out to do. Can't no one tell me I don't have discipline and drive. But this weight thing has me about licked. I'm almost ready to try the diet Melanie is on."

"What's that?"

"One of those high-protein diets. She won't even eat vegetables."

"Lord. But Carmel, you're a beautiful woman. I don't understand . . ."

"You can't completely understand. Look at Oprah. She's attractive, fabulously rich, successful, has a long-term relationship with a handsome man who's stayed by her side fat or thin, but still she said she felt that losing weight was her greatest accomplishment of all."

"She looks like she's gaining a little back. Boy, if I had that much money, I'd pay someone to diet for me and not worry about . . ."

"You're missing my point. *Oprah,* with all she had couldn't manage to be fat and happy. Now, how am I supposed to manage it?"

"And here I am wishing I had a little meat on my puny bones."

Carmel chuckled. "If I could think of a way to arrange the transfer, I'd give you all the meat your skinny heart desired."

"I've been wanting to tell you something."

"I'm sorry, Jasmine. I've been so much into myself with all that's going on. Is it something with the new man . . . What's his name—Keith?"

"Talk about ESP. How did you know it was about him?"

"Jasmine, with you it's always about some man."

"For the first time in my life I can say I'm truly in love."

"You've said that you were in love plenty of times. What about Michael?"

"Michael has always been there. He's like a habit. Probably one I need to outgrow. He was right there for me when I needed him. I didn't know what I would have done without him. I think that old sense of obligation still held me to him all these years."

"Are you sure it isn't love? Michael would have to love you to put up with all the stuff you put him through. And I've always thought that one day down deep in that cold, stony heart of yours you'd realize that you love him, too."

"I'm telling you that I realized I'm in love with Keith. He makes me feel . . . so alive and tingly. He's perfect, Carmel. Well, except for one little thing."

Carmel raised an eyebrow. "And what's that?"

"He's married."

There was a moment of silence.

"You are telling me that you're letting Michael go to be with some cheating married man?"

"His wife is frigid and she doesn't understand him."

Carmel burst out laughing. "You fell for the oldest line in history. Lord, have mercy. And you talk about me."

"You just don't understand. You don't understand about passion."

"If passion means acting like a fool, I don't think I want to understand."

Carmel waited for Jasmine's sharp retort, but it wasn't forthcoming. She heard a little choke over the phone and her eyes widened in disbelief. Jasmine sounding like she was going to cry was akin to the Pope looking like he was about to break into a song-and-dance routine.

"Geez Jas, I'm sorry. I'm starting to sound like my mother—critical, judgmental. I still don't think an affair with a married man is a good idea, but if you need to talk to someone, I'm here for you. It's not my job to judge."

Jasmine sniffed loudly. "I know I seem sort of flaky with men, but this feels different. I really care about him. I'm sure he'll leave his wife soon. He's got children. It takes time to get some things into place, that's all."

Carmel modulated her voice to remove any traces of admonition. "I sure hope things fall into place for you."

"It will. Everything is going to be great. I'm so happy to finally find love," Jasmine said. Her voice sounded anxious and more than a little worried, belying the meaning of her words.

"I'm glad for you," was all Carmel said.

Chapter 14

It was seven o'clock in the morning and the sky still had that early morning gray chill in the air. Carmel slammed the door of her Grand Am and headed for the Reynolds house for a badly needed infusion of coffee. She'd tossed and turned through the night, finally closing her eyes only to open them a bare second later to snarl at the chiming alarm clock.

She used her key to open the front door and heard the sound of the television. Marvin must be up and around, she thought as she strode toward the kitchen. She stopped to see if Marvin had his coffee already and pulled up short at the sight of Steve sitting by the couch browsing the newspaper. He smiled at her.

"Good morning Steve. I'm surprised to see you here in the morning," she said, grateful her voice was free of the trace of early morning fogginess.

"Got to take a day off sometimes. I thought I'd just hang around the house today and relax a bit."

The thought of having Steve around all day both

agitated and excited Carmel. "I'm going to get some coffee," she said.

"I just brewed a pot."

She poured herself a large mug. Worries about her children, Jasmine, the business and her diet failures were taking their toll. Insomnia was becoming the order of the day, or the night as it was.

Steve entered the kitchen and caught her in the middle of a yawn.

"Tired?" he asked.

"I didn't sleep well." She paused. "I think it's mainly my kids on my mind. Last week Jasmine and I thought that my son, Trey, might have been smoking in the house. And not tobacco either."

"Did you talk to him?"

"I tried. But he's only eleven. What if he doesn't even know what I'm talking about?"

"He'll know. Eleven is old enough to get into plenty of things."

Carmel bit her lip. "I'm going to talk to him."

The thought crossed her mind that she normally didn't confide in many people, but something about Steve had made her comfortable blurting out one of the foremost troubles on her mind. It had nothing to do with the considerable sexual attraction she felt for him. There was something about him that let her know that he would care. That he really wanted to know why she was tired and what was going on in her life, that he wasn't just mouthing a trite greeting. And he listened with his coffee-brown eyes intent on hers, drinking up every word.

How many men had ever really listened to her? Not many. She could tell their minds were on what they were going to say next rather than what she was saying. But in the most minor interactions, it felt as if Steve came outside himself and transcended his own ego and was really there for her. She supposed women had fallen in love with him just because of that trait.

"What sort of things does your son like to do?"

"Excuse me?" Carmel said, jarred out of her reverie.

"I was curious about what sort of things Trey likes to do."

"Oh. He likes computers, computer games, dinosaurs, astronomy, superheroes, things of that sort."

"Does he have any interest in sports or athletics?"

"No. My daughter Melanie is the athlete in the family. Trey is the academic one, a budding computer nerd and proud of it."

"Nothing wrong with that. But this culture is so sports-oriented. It starts up and gets worse at that age. A kid could start feeling bad about himself if sports aren't his thing."

Something in his voice caused Carmel to meet his eyes. She discerned a shadow of some long-ago pain in them. "Were you into sports?"

"Not at all. I was one of those kids that an argument started over which team captain would have to take me. I was the skinniest boy in class, and although it was before the term came into popularity, nerd would have been the perfect word to describe me."

"Really?" she asked, tipping her head to peer up at all six-foot plus of him.

"I caught up with a vengeance when I hit sixteen. I got into basketball and started taking an interest in sports for the first time in my life. You can't believe what a difference it made to my high school social life. I went from ignored outcast to the golden boy overnight."

"I never would have guessed you were ever an outcast."

"Four-eyed shrimp was what they'd call me. I told

myself it didn't matter because I was smarter than all of them. But it did matter. A lot."

She was silent for a moment, taking in that this handsome, acclaimed physician was once on the outside looking in.

"You think it would make a difference if Trey was involved in sports?"

"With what you're worried about? Probably not. But I think it would make a difference if some older male took an interest in him."

"You're talking about a role model. It's true, Trey has had no black men he's been all that close to. We're a household of females."

"I'm on the board of this organization that mentors young people, pairing them with an older person who will take an interest in their lives. I believe it makes a difference."

Carmel nodded thoughtfully over her cup of steaming coffee. "It might."

"I'd like to meet Trey if that's all right with you. Maybe we could take in a game."

"That's generous of you. I'll talk to Trey. I think he would love it."

Carmel leaned toward Steve, excited about the prospect of her son getting a positive black male role model. It had been something she had been worried about for quite a while. Then all he did was touch her cheek. It was only a small, imperceptible movement, more like a brush than a caress. She drew in a quick breath. She'd forgotten how dangerous it was to get too close to him. She looked up and met his eyes, and right at that moment, everything changed.

She knew, she just knew that he wanted her right then. It didn't matter how much she weighed or what she looked like. All that mattered was that she was a woman and he was a man, and their bodies would fit together . . . so perfectly.

"Good," Steve said.

There was a space of silence between them. It wasn't an awkward silence, but one full of unspoken meaning. Carmel felt as if she was on the brink of some momentous happening. She was hanging on for dear life, afraid to fall off.

Steve broke the silence first. "I'd like to take him out with me Saturday afternoon. I'll give you a call. By then you should have spoken to him."

"Okay," she said. She turned away and poured herself another cup of coffee. She'd just given Steve entree into her private life. She could feel herself slipping, falling . . . falling into—

"Thank you," she told him. "You have no idea how much this means to me."

The housekeeper had left early, and Carmel had just finished up the dishes when she heard the doorbell ring. A few minutes later she heard Marvin calling for her. She wiped her hands on the dishtowel. When she got into the den, she saw Steve deep in conversation with the physical therapist who looked like Halle Berry's twin. She stared up at him, the adoration in her eyes evident from across the room. A little rock landed in the pit of Carmel's stomach, quickly followed by another. What she wouldn't give to look like that.

"There you are," Marvin said to her. "Would you go and get me a fresh cup of coffee. Make a fresh pot. The cup I just drank tasted stale."

Carmel picked up his coffee cup, restraining an urge to reply, *Yassum, Massah*. She darted a look at Steve and the physical therapist. Steve was intent on what the woman was saying in the attentive way he usually was. The physical therapist was talking, gesticulating animatedly. The woman licked her lips when she met his eyes like he was a lollipop and she wanted to give him a lick.

The witch, Carmel thought. She knew she was the one being female doggish, if only in her thoughts, but she couldn't help it. The physical therapist looked good, no doubt about it. She'd never thought of herself as the jealous type, but the idea of Steve alone with that woman made her feel a little sick inside.

Steve looked good with that woman. They looked right together. That was the type who would be at his side, not some heavy-bodied woman like Carmel. What had she been thinking this morning, getting all dreamy-eyed and gloppy-hearted because Steve said he wanted to take an interest in her son? So what? He did a lot of charity work in the community, and Carmel seemed to fall under that category with a capital C.

She'd take what he offered for her son, but she'd put a brake on herself and her emotions. If she kept going the way she was, she would figuratively fall flat on her cushioned rear right in front of him. Sometimes pride was the best thing she had. If she lost the ability to hold her head high and know that she would never make a fool out of herself, she'd have lost everything.

The physical therapist's giggle mixed with the drip, drip of coffee from the coffeemaker. Obviously, the woman was having a good time. She heard Marvin's gruff laugh joining in. It made it worse that Marvin liked the therapist, too. His words still stung, "Carmel, if you looked like that girl you'd have it made."

She couldn't disagree with him. If she looked like that, the world would be hers. She sure wouldn't be working as a physical therapist. She'd fantasized a life more along the lines of Sienna Lake. She'd get the credentials for some man to put her in charge of something important. Magazine layouts, public acclaim, flashbulbs popping. *Skreeeetch.* The sound of a needle scratching over a record echoed in her mind. She knew that sound. It meant—

Whoa baby, time out, full stop, that other voice in her head echoed. *So, you're saying that all slim, attractive women who are in positions of importance got there because some man put them there?* The voice sounded more than a little pissed. *Pleeeze. Are you perpetuating the myth that women aren't capable of doing it on their own? That if a woman looks good, she can't have the brains to match? You're just jealous. Jealous, do you hear me? You'd like to pull out every strand of that woman's hair and Steve's ex-wife's too. How small of you, how petty and mean . . .* The voice faded into the background.

The voice was right. She hated to admit it, but the damn thing was usually right. She felt a pang of envy when she thought of Steve's ex-wife. She was professionally and personally acclaimed for her beauty, smarts and know-how. Steve Reynolds had loved her and her witch of a mother-in-law, Donna, had liked her, too. That's the way it went with all the slim and beautiful women in the world.

The voice in her head rumbled again. *There you go again. Quit it, I say. Quit it.*

The coffee was finally done. She poured a cup and walked back into the den. The therapist must have had a very short session. Now she was draped over the arm of the couch, still giggling at something. Marvin was back in his recliner grinning broadly. Everyone was getting along so well.

Carmel set the cup on the end table next to Marvin. "I think I'd like to go home a little early. Steve?"

Steve hesitated a little. Carmel dared him to say no. If he said that, this would be her last day and at this rate she wouldn't be overly regretful.

"Sure," Steve said, drawing out the word a little too long. "I guess I'll see you tomorrow. Take care."

Marvin looked at Carmel searchingly. "You sure you're all right?"

"I'm okay. The diet must have my nerves frayed."

Carmel felt the physical therapist eye her. She glanced at her and saw the woman primp, running her hand over her slim hip. Carmel supposed she was proud of herself. She'd bet she was one of those women who jumped up at the first crack of dawn to run up and down the street in the rain, snow, ice and wind. Carmel always watched those women with a touch of astonishment and envy. She wondered how they maintained their self-discipline and devotion to their bodies. Her life always got in the way.

Everyday living tripped her up. She couldn't stick to a diet unless she thought of it every waking moment. An exercise program was beyond her capability unless it was the number one priority in her life. But she had kids, a job, a home, laundry . . . All those other things got in the way. *If getting small was all that important to you, you'd make like the commercial said and just do it,* that irritating voice in her head noted.

"Would you shut up?" she snapped. Then she looked around hurriedly to see if anyone was in earshot. On top of everything, she seemed to be losing a marble or two. Having mental arguments with herself was one thing, but answering herself was a little much. Maybe it was sour grapes. Maybe it was wrong to feel entitled to it all. But that's what she wanted. She wanted it all. And Steve Reynolds would be the icing on the cake.

Chapter 15

Carmel and Melanie were locked in an uneasy truce. Melanie promised to include vegetables in her diet and Carmel promised to lay off what Melanie ate or didn't eat. Her daughter's outbursts had never been discussed.

"Fat and ugly and all alone just like you." Carmel almost couldn't bear to think about it, much less talk about it.

When Carmel entered the den, Melanie was sprawled in front of the TV. Her daughter didn't look up. It gave Carmel a little pang. Once her daughter would've bounded over, heedless of the television program, chattering about her day. Now, all there was was sullen silence.

"Where's Trey?"

"He said he was going out with his boys."

"His boys?"

"Yeah. You know, his buddies."

"It's almost dinnertime. When did he say he was going to get back?"

"Oh. I forgot to tell you he said he wouldn't be in for dinner."

"He *said* he won't be in for dinner? Where is he? He knows better than that."

"I don't know. All he said was that he was going out with his boys and he would be in after dinner. He said they had something to do."

"Uh-uh. No way." Carmel put her hands on her hips and fumed. "Tell me what friends he's out with. I have some phone calls to some parents to make."

"I don't know!"

"Out with it."

"Mom, it's none of my business." Melanie jumped to her feet and ran up the stairs toward her room, Carmel hot on her heels. "Leave me alone!" Melanie cried.

Carmel heard the front door open. "What's going on? What's all that noise?" Carmel heard her mother say.

The door slammed to Melanie's room. Carmel wheeled and retreated.

"Were you chasing that child?" Mama asked.

"I don't know what's gotten into her. Both of them. She gives me this message that Trey's going to miss dinner because he's out with his boys."

"His boys?"

"Yeah, his boys. And then she went off on me when I asked her who his boys were," Carmel said.

Mama got that look in her eyes that she remembered so well. It was that look that meant she had had enough and somebody was going to catch hell and it wasn't going to be her. "I've paid the cost to be the boss," Mama used to say.

She watched her mother climb the stairs to Melanie's room. She sank into a living room chair, feeling frustrated and angry. She had tried so hard with her children, and with the merest whiff of hormones, all went to hell in a handbasket. Where was Trey? Was he out with some gang? Couldn't be at eleven years old. And Melanie had been transformed seemingly overnight from a pleasant, friendly kid to a sullen and insecure teenager.

Carmel couldn't really analyze her reaction to her mother coming in and taking her wayward child in hand. At thirteen, she'd been far worse than Melanie, and it had seemed back then that her mother was far more interested in her own problems than what happened to Carmel. But time passes, things change.

It was only a few moments later when Melanie came down the stairs looking chastened, followed by Mama.

"What do you have to say to your mother, young lady?" Mama asked.

"I'm sorry for mouthing off at you. And I don't know who Trey went out with."

Carmel nodded. "I don't know why you think you have call to disrespect me all of a sudden. I can't imagine what's gotten into you," her voice trailed away. "Please go to your room. I'll call you out for dinner."

Melanie went back up the stairs without a backward glance.

"Thanks Mama," Carmel said, sinking back into the chair and rubbing her forehead with her hand. "It's true what I told Melanie. It's like something possessed them both all of a sudden. I don't know quite how to handle this all. I'm worried sick about Trey."

"Ain't nothing wrong with Trey a good butt-whipping won't cure. You've spoiled that boy rotten. Now, Melanie, what's wrong with her is just the normal course of things." Her mother arched a brow at her. "You were worse."

"I know, Mama. I know."

They had just finished up dinner when Trey walked in. Silence fell. Mama got up out of her chair and started clearing the table. "Talk to him Carmel, I'll take care of the dishes. And don't forget what I said." Mama looked at her meaningfully. Carmel stifled a sigh. Somehow she doubted that giving Trey a good butt-whipping would make a whole lot of difference except make him surly and more rebellious. She hadn't spanked Trey since he was eight.

"Trey come with me." Her son looked young and scared, like a little boy. It was hard to confront him with her worst suspicions. They sounded ridiculous even to her. What if she was wrong? Would she be putting ideas in his head?

"I feel like grounding you at least until you're thirty. What possessed you to think you could go hang out with your friends and be gone past dinner without asking me directly? Do you realize how worried I've been about you?"

"I had to go, Mom. My boys gave me no choice."

"And what is this about your boys at eleven years old? Are you talking about some sort of gang?"

"I guess so. They're my friends. Last year I didn't have very many friends."

"Trey, I want you to have friends. But that's not the point. The point is that you were out of the house without permission and I didn't know where you were."

"But you don't understand. The other kids used to make fun of me because I was so small. Well now

I'm bigger and I've got friends. I don't want to lose my friends.''

"Baby, I don't want you to lose your friends either. But friends have nothing to do with following the rules of this house. You're a child in my care and I will not have you leaving this house without knowing where you are, and I will not have you out in the streets after dark.''

"I can't be a baby. All of the other boys could meet down at the bowling alley. You treat me like a baby. It's not fair!''

"Regardless of what you think is fair, you're eleven years old. And you're grounded for a month.''

"Mom!'' He looked like he was going to cry. It was all Carmel could do not to capitulate to him. "I'm going to lose all my friends. They're going to think I'm stuck up or something, never coming out to play or to hang out with them.''

"Sorry, but those are the consequences. Come on down and I'll fix you a plate.''

Trey put on a tragic face and marched slowly down to the dining room in front of her.

Carmel rinsed the dishes and handed them to her mother, who loaded them in the dishwasher. "Where's Jasmine?'' her mom asked. "It's unusual when I don't see her here around dinnertime.''

"Jasmine's got a new man.''

"What was wrong with the old one?''

"Nothing, but the new man is apparently better.''

"If he feeds her and keeps her home on a weekday, I guess he is.''

"Michael works long hours during the week, and this man only wants to look like he works long hours. He's married.''

Mama crossed to the sink and wiped her hands on a dishtowel. "Jasmine's not going to be a fine little thing forever. She needs to settle down instead of trying to run down some sorry-ass man."

"Michael and she have been together since high school. He's been there for her ever since her family was killed. He's the one she needs to settle down with."

"Sometimes a woman can't see her nose because she's looking too hard at the pimple on the end of it. I'm happy you're settled and put your priorities on your family instead of some man."

Carmel walked over to the coffeepot and poured herself a cup of coffee. "Want some?"

"Thanks. Do you have anything sweet?"

"Nothing but some Fig Newtons."

"I hate Fig Newtons."

"So do I. That's why I bought them. I wanted to have something sweet for Trey in the house."

"So how's your diet doing?"

"Not too good. Did I tell you what Melanie said to me a few days ago? She said she wanted to lose weight because she didn't want to be fat and ugly and alone like I am."

Her mother didn't say anything, just took another sip of coffee.

"Sometimes I envy Jasmine. She enjoys a part of life I don't seem to have access to."

"Your daughter is thirteen years old. In case you forgot the hell age thirteen can be for girls, let me remind you. I don't see that you can put any call in anything Melanie said. She was mad and she was trying to hurt you."

Carmel sighed. "Mama, that's the point. She did hurt me."

"Sometimes I wonder when you are going to grow

up. You know you're going to have to sometime to be able to raise these kids right.''

"That's just like you, Mama. I confided in you and all you can do is spout off your opinion and put me down. You never try to understand how I feel. You never really listen.''

"That's because you seldom make any sense.''

"I'm going to my room.''

"Famous last words, familiar, too.''

Carmel shook with anger as she shut the door to her room behind her. Sometimes when she really thought her mother had changed, that they were finally getting the close mother-daughter relationship she'd always hoped for, she'd realize that Mama never changed at all. It made her mad and sad all at the same time.

Chapter 16

"Trey, hurry up! He's going to be here any minute now." Carmel rushed to the window one more time to see if Steve's black Mercedes was in sight.

Her heart jumped as his car pulled up in front of the house. "Trey, c'mon. He's here," she yelled.

She was far more excited than her son was. Still sulking over his punishment, he was decidedly nonenthusiastic about this afternoon's outing. The doorbell rang and Carmel started to run to the door. She pulled up and wiped her moist palms on her jeans. "Chill, be cool girl," she muttered to herself.

Then Steve stood there, looking so good that she wanted to take a bite out of him. "Come in," she said, standing to the side.

He smiled at her, looking both eager and endearingly nervous. "Where's Trey?" he asked, looking around.

"He's still up in his room. Hold on, I'll run up and get him."

Oh, Lord, those flutters in her tummy felt like date

jitters. Get it through your head, this is no date, no outing for you and Dr. Steve Reynolds to merely enjoy each other's company. It's a charity thing for him. A nice guy holding out a helping hand, that's all.

When she got to Trey's room, he was lying on his bed staring at the ceiling. Carmel's lips tightened. "Trey, I told you to come on. Steve is here."

"All right." He got up dispiritedly from the bed.

"Hold up, young man. I hope you know better than to walk down the stairs acting like you've gone crazy. What's wrong with you?"

"I don't want to go."

"Why not? You don't even know Steve."

"That's right. I don't know him and I'd rather be with my friends."

Carmel leaned down and met Trey's eyes. "I'm asking you," begging you, she thought to herself "to please give this a chance. We'll talk about you being grounded later, but for now let's go out and have a good time."

"Okay," Trey mumbled, rubbing the toe of his tennis shoe in the carpet.

Carmel prayed that it would be all right. She prayed that Trey wouldn't act a fool and Steve would like him.

Carmel made brief introductions. Trey looked at Steve out of the corner of his eyes, avoiding direct eye contact. Then he saw Steve's black Mercedes, and his eyes widened. "That car's phat, man," he said.

Steve looked puzzled for a moment before he comprehended Trey's meaning. "Thanks," he replied. Trey squeezed into the little back seat. He was quiet, but Carmel felt his sullen attitude fade away, much to her relief. He seemed content to look out the window at the passing cars.

A comfortable silence descended over them. She

didn't have anything to say except questions about the outing Steve had planned. She decided she wasn't going to ask him anything, but let things happen as they happened. She'd relax and enjoy letting someone else take care of the arrangements for once. Don't worry, be happy, she thought to herself, pushing her nervousness at meeting Steve's friends from her mind. His sleek machine swallowed the miles.

When they arrived, she heard the beat of the music before she saw the people. Their voices and laughter rose over the heavy bass thump of boom boxes playing old school funk. The CD blared George Clinton's voice as he declared, *"Make my funk the P-Funk, I want my funk uncut."*

A group of guys played basketball at a nearby court. Another knot of men stood court over a giant brick barbecue. Carmel's mouth watered at the smell and the sight of pork and beef steaks, chicken quarters and slabs of ribs roasting.

"Trey!" a voice called. A boy with a baseball glove in his hand ran up to them. "Hey, dawg," Trey said as they touched their fists together.

Dawg? Carmel wondered. Where does he get this stuff, some rap record? He was way too young . . .

"We're going to play some ball. Want to come?" the boy asked.

Trey looked at her, and she nodded. Trey and the boy ran over to a group of kids standing on a nearby baseball diamond.

Steve led her to a brightly colored tent that covered tables laden with food. "I want you to meet somebody," he said.

A hefty woman, bigger than Carmel, stood court over a table of foil-wrapped dishes. When she spied Steve, she whooped and rushed over to him.

"How you doing, baby?" she cried as she hugged

him enthusiastically. He picked her up and swung her around. No mean feat, Carmel thought, eyeing the woman.

"Aunt Vicky, this is Carmel Matthews. Carmel, meet my favorite aunt."

"I'm your only aunt, boy," she said, chuckling.

This must be Marvin's sister, Carmel thought. She couldn't imagine anyone seeming more the opposite of Donna, Steve's mother. The woman's cocoa face was warm and welcoming. Her smile seemed to invite you to plop down and pour out your troubles in a long heart-to-heart with her.

"How's my sister doing? I heard her husband isn't doing too well."

"Mom's doing fine and she hasn't said a word about Gene. What's going on?"

"That's strange she hasn't said anything to you. The man just had a heart attack. A minor one, but still . . ."

Steve's eyebrow arched. "She's been at the house almost every day."

Now Vicky looked taken aback. "I heard there were some problems in my sister's home, but I paid no mind because I'd heard second-hand. You know Donna doesn't have anything to say to me."

She looked over at Carmel and pulled a set of keys from her pocket. "See that blue van over there? Could you go and get the baked beans out of the back seat? I'd sure appreciate it."

Carmel took her time because the errand had been an obvious ploy. Steve and his aunt were deep in conversation, their heads close together. She leaned against the van and closed her eyes. What a perfect day. The air was fragrant, warm and mellow with a faint overlay of the tang of fall. A soft breeze ruffled her hair. Then she heard a screech of brakes and Carmel's eyes snapped open.

A flashy red Corvette convertible pulled up and a slim African-American woman got out, her back to her. The woman's black hair fell over her shoulders like silk. A weave, Carmel thought, but a good one. Carmel admired how the woman managed to exit the low-slung car gracefully with a skirt so short. Then she turned and Carmel drew in a breath at the sight of the woman's burnished bronze features. Sienna Lake.

Sienna made a beeline straight to Steve and Vicky. Carmel saw they were still intent on their conversation and they didn't look up until she had almost reached them. Sienna threw herself against Steve and wrapped her arms around his neck. He rocked a little, obviously surprised and off balance. Then his ex-wife pulled his head down and pressed her lips against his.

Steve disengaged himself and looked toward the blue van, beckoning Carmel to come over. With a small sense of satisfaction that Sienna's enthusiastic greeting had obviously backfired, she got out the baked beans and walked toward them.

"Sienna, I want you to meet Carmel," Steve said, pulling her to his side. Vicky took the baked beans from Carmel with a small smile.

Sienna looked Carmel up and down, then gave her a dismissive glance and turned her attention back to Steve. "Honey, I have wonderful news," she purred to him.

"What is it?"

"It's private." She cast a glance over at Vicky. "Very private. It's going to change everything between us."

Steve raised an eyebrow. "Oh, yeah?" he asked, his voice skeptical.

"Yes. Something we both wanted more than anything. I'll tell you everything over Sunday brunch."

"Not tomorrow. Give me a call at my office. Maybe I can take a few minutes off Wednesday."

She stuck her lower lip out. "I have to talk to you before then. I told you it was important."

Steve shrugged. "That's the earliest I have free."

The woman actually stamped her foot, Carmel observed in disbelief. Geez, that was a move she wouldn't dare make in public after the age of eight.

"I see you haven't changed a bit," Sienna announced, still pouting. And with a fling of her hair, she marched back to her convertible, got in, slammed the door and peeled out.

"That woman drives me nuts," Steve murmured.

"She's full of herself, that's for sure," Vicky said. "Aren't you even a little curious about what she wanted to tell you?"

"Not really. I doubt it'll amount to much. Sienna likes to play games."

He smiled at Carmel. "Do you want to go watch the kids?" he asked, nodding toward the baseball diamond.

"I need her here to help me put out all this food," Vicky said. "You get on and let us get to work."

"Yes, go on. I'll be over later," Carmel said. She liked Steve's aunt already and felt at ease in her presence.

"You know what to set aside for me," he told Vicky. He strode away whistling.

"What's he want you to set aside?"

"My rolls. He knows I brought a batch of my rolls I make from scratch. My grandmother's recipe, they're light as a feather and they go fast."

"Sounds great," Carmel said, her feelings mixed as she eyed the platters of side dishes and rich desserts.

"You start over that way and set up the dessert table," Vicky directed.

Great, just great, Carmel thought. She got to set up the dessert table. That would be the icing on the cake. She was holding on to this diet by her finger-nails. From the smell of that barbecue and the look of those desserts, she was going to fall flat on her big behind.

"Are you and my mom good friends, or are you just her boss?" Trey asked Steve.

Steve hesitated a moment before answering. "I'm her boss and I hope we are good friends. I'd like to maybe be more than that."

Trey digested this for a moment. "You want to be her boyfriend?" he asked.

Steve nodded.

"Cool," Trey said, a grin breaking out on his brown face.

"Don't tell your mom I said that. You know how funny girls get," Steve said in a conspiratorial man-to-man whisper.

"Tell me about it. Mom gets pretty funny, especially lately."

Steve raised an eyebrow and opened his mouth to ask funny how. But then he spied Carmel strolling up with two plates in her hands.

"Having a good time, little guy?" she asked Trey, handing him a plate.

He nodded. "Mom, can I go eat with the other kids?"

"Sure, baby."

A quick wave and grin and he was gone.

Steve bit into a rib with a sigh of satisfaction. "Umm, this is good. Where's your plate?"

"I'll get one later. I already had a few ribs. They're really good."

"You look more relaxed than I've seen you in weeks. The outdoors seems to suit you," Steve said.

"I'm having a good time. I've met some interesting people. Your aunt is great, really funny."

Carmel sat down at the picnic table next to him. "She is, isn't she? We've always been pretty close. She's easier to talk to than my mother." Now, that was an understatement, Steve thought to himself.

"You have a lot of family here?" she asked.

"No, not really. Aunt Vicky is my mother's only sibling. She has a couple of kids but none of them live here. Dad has two brothers, but they live out of state also. What about you?"

"Mom has several sisters and brothers, but they're not that close. I see the family usually only on holidays."

Silence fell between them as Steve concentrated on his ribs. He was hungry. One of the many things he liked about Carmel was how she'd let him eat without feeling the obligation to keep the flow of conversation going.

Satisfied, he wiped his fingers with a napkin and looked down at her curve of shoulder and neck, covered by a light blue T-shirt. Her hair fell over her shoulders and glinted with reddish highlights in the sunshine. He reached for her and touched, first lightly massaging her neck, then harder, his surgeon's hands deftly seeking taut muscles. She felt as good as he thought she would. At first she tensed under his fingers, then she relaxed and sighed with pleasure.

"I've noticed you've been tense the last few weeks. Anything on your mind?" he asked.

"Nothing except the usual. Family stuff, mainly, the kids."

"Maybe you don't get away enough. Take time for yourself."

"That's probably right. But—"

"No buts. Let's go out tonight. A good leisurely meal, some soft jazz, pure relaxation."

She looked up at him from under the curl of her long lashes. "Are you asking me on a date, Dr. Reynolds?"

"Sure am, and if you mention a word about charity or gratitude, I'll . . ."

"You'll what?"

"I won't give you another neck massage."

"Mmmmm. Now that's cruel punishment." She laughed, a sexy contralto ripple, and he wanted to kiss her then and there.

"Tonight then?" he asked.

"Tonight," she answered.

Chapter 17

The waiter solicitously filled Carmel's wineglass. She sipped, feeling pure satisfaction. Steve had said relaxation was what he had in mind and the evening thus far had been as smooth as soft velvet and just as pleasurable.

She looked out at the twinkling lights of Atlanta, which brightly glittered below the slowly revolving restaurant on top of the hotel.

"You looked like a contented cat, the way you just stretched."

She darted a glance at Steve and smiled a little. "I was just thinking about what a good time I was having. Thanks for asking me. You're right about me needing to get out and take my mind off things . . ." her voice trailed away.

The waiter came to sweep away the leavings of their feast, the remains of lobster dripping with butter. The meal had been rich and delicious, but Carmel didn't worry about the calories. She could hardly believe she was sitting here in this wonderful restaurant with this fabulous man. She felt like a princess from a fairy tale.

Her African Prince smiled at her. "Once we're done with this bottle of wine, there's this group playing jazz downstairs. The pianist is a friend of mine. He just sent me his latest CD. I think it's his best yet."

Carmel ran her finger around the edge of her wineglass. Steve looked deep into her eyes and a shiver ran up her spine.

"That was the plan anyway," he continued. "I like to listen to music but right now I'm enjoying talking to you more. It's amazing even though our backgrounds are completely different how many experiences we have in common."

"Difficult family is rather universal." They had been talking about their mothers. She had no idea how they got on that topic, but it had occupied more than half of their mealtime. Carmel had the advantage of meeting Steve's mother and she could truly empathize with his difficulties with the woman.

The problems with her own mother were less cut-and-dried. Her mother fit the stereotype of the semi-heroic strong black woman raising her child alone. Maybe being an only child made the mother-daughter dynamics more difficult, Carmel thought. She loved her mother dearly, but half the time wanted to strangle her. It wasn't that her mother was all that controlling or even particularly demanding, it was that she was so damn opinionated. She was so free with her advice and her judgments whether they were asked for or not. But that wasn't the main problem between them. The problem was the wounds of the past that never quite went away and were never discussed. Never.

"You're looking pensive all the sudden," Steve said.

"Just thinking about mothers and daughters. Melanie and I used to get along so well. But it seemed like as soon as she hit thirteen, something moved in and possessed her. Everything changed between us overnight. We went from friends to antagonists and I can't figure out why." She frowned, worry filling her.

Steve lifted the wine bottle and refilled her glass. "Maybe it's time to put the discussion of family on ice. I'd much rather talk about you."

"Me?"

"You know I'm utterly fascinated with you."

Carmel thought she was going to choke on her wine. "No, I didn't realize that," she managed to answer.

"Whenever I'm with you, sometimes I can tell when you're worried, but still you exhibit an atmosphere of . . . of peace, nurturing. Something like that."

"I'm a regular earth mother," Carmel said.

"I didn't mean like that. I meant you're someone who naturally makes people feel comfortable. You have no idea what a rare quality that is."

A warm feeling settled deep in Carmel's stomach. She leaned toward him and moistened her lips. He reached down and touched her hand, pulling it toward him. He rotated his thumb around the middle of her palm in a slow, lazy circle. She met his gaze and started to drown. She sank into the warm brown depths of his eyes, sank in like they were quicksand. There was no hope of rescue and she didn't particularly want to be saved, she realized as she happily went under.

She wanted this man more than she wanted anything in the world, and his eyes said he wanted her. *Once-in-a-lifetime, once-in-a-lifetime,* she heard the voice in her head say. *Go for it, Carmel. Go for it.* She pictured herself standing in front of an icy blue pool on a sweltering day. Would she ease into the frigid water or would she jump in and get the shock over quickly?

She jumped.

"I really like this hotel. I've often fantasized about having a room here. I can see it like something out of the movies, one of those soft-filtered scenes. One of those romantic interludes complete with champagne, strawberries and soft violin music," she said.

The splash of her dive echoed in her mind. There it lay in between them, the invitation subtly spoken but clear as a bell. Carmel waited for his reaction, trying not to shiver from the shock of her daring.

Something burned in his eyes now, something primitive. More than admiration, more than mere desire. He wanted her with all the primal urges of a man wanting a woman. Every drop of femininity within her responded in kind.

"I think I can arrange that," he said.

"I wish you would." Carmel could hardly believe the words coming from her mouth were hers. But then she'd gone without for so long. Steve was like a candy bowl in front of a starving person; Hershey's kisses, preferably unwrapped, dark chocolate and melt-in-your-mouth luscious.

"Check, please," Steve said, his eyes never leaving hers.

As they rose from the table, Steve came close and touched her arm. Heat radiated from him. She shivered inside. His hand fit perfectly in the small of her back. She had no desire to think—she only wanted to feel. A strange and different mood descended over her, reckless desire, abandoned passion, wanton need.

It seemed like only a moment passed and then she

was in the hotel room listening to the door click behind them. She walked into his arms without hesitation. His head bent and his lips hungrily devoured hers. Their tongues mingled in a passionate dance, tasting, wanting, and craving more. The length of his hard body pressed against hers and their clothes seemed to be a heavy barrier between them, dragging them away from their passion.

Hands touched skin, at first tentatively, then feverishly pushing clothes aside. Flesh against flesh. His hands trailed fire. She was on fire, burning. They fell on the bed, their clothes discarded. She cared about nothing but the inferno within her and the intoxication of the man who promised to quench it.

His lips grazed her neck and over her breasts. Then she gasped from the sweet sensation of his warm mouth against her, his tongue rotating, caressing . . . Fire. She couldn't think. She was reduced to a primitive being, craving only to be joined.

His fingers explored her secret crevices, then his tongue. She didn't care in her abandon, it felt so good, so sweet. Soft murmurs and moans, incoherent and needing. She wanted . . . she wanted more. A groan came from deep within her and she arched up against him. "Now," she whispered. "Please." She reached for him.

"Yes," he murmured.

She heard the tear of foil and a moment later he slid up her body. She felt the silky column of his hardness. Yes. She clasped her hands behind his back and wrapped her thighs around his waist, open, hot, slick, wet and ready for him. He entered her with one smooth thrust that racked her with pleasure, painful in its intensity.

He moved within her and she moved with him. He filled her up to the brink with all she wanted and more. Silky, smooth friction that felt like heaven. Tender and slow at first, savoring the sensations, then quickening as passion overtook them. She quivered inside, trembling, racing for the edge of the precipice. Faster, harder. They pounded each other, breath coming in short gasps.

Her head lashed from side to side, her fingers scratched and pulled at the sheets. Incoherent moans, oh God, oh God, oh God. She fell over the edge. Crashing, she hit bottom and for a moment she thought she was dying. Crashed again and again until she heard herself crying, begging for mercy.

She came back to herself in time to meet him. She met his deep thrust, his moan, and held him while he stiffened, his entire body jerking imperceptibly. They subsided together, moist, breath still coming fast.

He pushed her damp curls aside and pressed his lips against her temple. "You're so beautiful," he whispered softly in her ear.

Chapter 18

Carmel awoke with a start, aware of a heavy leg thrown over her thigh, a masculine arm thrown possessively over her stomach. Her naked stomach. Flashback to the heated passion of last night. Ohmigod. She tried to move her arm to peer at her watch, but it didn't work. She slid away from Steve. She held her breath and willed him not to move. He muttered and turned when she moved his arm away from her. She froze.

He quieted and she exhaled silently in relief, retrieving her scattered clothes by feel and retreating to the bathroom. Once the door was shut securely behind her, she flipped on the light and looked at her watch. It was 2:15 A.M. Her mother and children would be frantic.

Carmel hurriedly washed up and pulled on her clothes. Catching a glance of her face in the mirror, she drew in her breath quickly at the sight—smudged makeup, heavy-lidded eyes, swollen lips, disheveled hair. She looked obviously and thoroughly made love to.

She wanted to bury her face in her hands and fall, crying and howling to the floor. How could she have done it? But she knew how. That spell of drugged, heated passion caused by a man she wanted so bad she could taste it was how. Embers from the flames of his passion still glowed within her. She licked her lips and tasted him. Satiation infused her, making her feel . . . utterly feminine, womanly, a feeling she'd denied herself for too long.

If she could run away and never see him again, she'd raise her chin and go on. Running wasn't the answer, but what was? He was . . . perfect, so perfect. He'd filled her up, and given her all she wanted. They'd met each other with equal passion. So why did she feel so . . . so ashamed? So bad? They made love. Made love, that was all.

What did love have to do with it? An annoying voice in her mind whispered, *For him, probably nothing, but face it, for you it meant everything.*

That was the reason she felt so bad and good at the same time. She wanted, needed, maybe even loved Steve Reynolds and he didn't love her back. Was she nothing but a convenient receptacle to slake his passions?

That annoying voice rumbled, *Woman, you are way past grown and you wanted it as much as he did, probably more,* it admonished her. *Get past the mind games and self-recrimination. Suck it up and go ahead and do what you got to do. Live your life and look him straight in the eye the next time you see him and smile. Hold your head up and never, never lose your pride.* Carmel bit her lip as the lecturing voice finally fell. It was right. She asked for it and she got it. Why should she want more than what was on the menu?

Later that morning, home in her own bed, the shrill ring of the phone jarred her awake. She fumbled on the bedside table next to her and picked it up on the next ring. "Hello?" she said, her voice fogged with sleep.

"Carmel, I woke up and you weren't beside me." Steve's voice wasn't accusing or angry, simply flat and matter-of-fact.

Her mouth felt filled with sandpaper, raspy and raw. She had no idea what to say.

"Carmel?" she heard Steve say when the silence had drawn out too long.

"I was worried about my children. You were sleeping so soundly I didn't want to wake you." *Coward,* that hateful little voice inside her head muttered.

"I wouldn't have minded. Though I would have tried to talk you into making a call to your family and staying to share breakfast with me."

"Ummmmm."

"You sound sexy. What are your plans for later this day?"

Her heart leaped, then just as quickly settled somewhere down into the pit of her stomach. No. She couldn't drag this out. She didn't know if she'd be able to face the pain of falling deeper into the snare and not being able to climb out. She couldn't be with him and want more than he could ever give to someone like her.

Someone like her. A cold, leaden feeling descended. "I've got some things I need to do," she answered.

"Okay. I'll see you Monday then?"

Was that disappointment she heard in his voice? "I'll be at work Monday."

"All right. I guess I'll let you go. But, Carmel?"

"Yes?"

"I had a really good time last night and I hope you did, too."

She couldn't lie to the man. "I had a good time."

Her hand shook a little when she hung up the phone. He'd wanted to see her again. But what did he expect now? A weekday nooner quickie to relieve the tension of a hard day in surgery? Not from her, no matter how much she wanted it also. Steve Reynolds was like a potato chip. She couldn't eat just one.

Her mother gave her an arch glance as she entered the kitchen. "Missed you last night."

"Yeah, we were out pretty late."

"Did you have a good time?"

"A very good time."

"Uh-huh. I bet he had a good time, too."

Carmel's head whipped around and she stared at her mother. "What do you mean by that?"

"You got that just-been-bedded look in your eye. That look ain't been there so long, it's kinda hard to miss. I only hope you know what you're doing."

"Whatever I'm doing, it's no business of yours." The words slipped out of her mouth before she could stop them.

"Excuse me? I don't care how old you think you are, I'm still your mama. You'd best watch your mouth."

Carmel licked her lips. The old habit of backing down to her mother was still strong. "What I'm saying is what concern is it of yours what Steve and I did last night?"

"He's your employer. And it's foolhardy to let a man like that get in your pants. That doctor isn't in your league and you know it. When your foolishness backfires, you're not only going to get hurt, your children may feel the backlash. That's why I'm concerned."

Carmel literally bit her tongue to keep it from lashing out at her mother. Anger roiled and boiled just under her skin. It was one thing for her to think it, but another for her mother to voice it.

"Are you telling me you have a problem with a man wanting me? That a handsome, successful doctor is out of my league?" She whispered the words.

Her mother was silent.

Moments ticked by and the anger silently exploded through Carmel's skin. "You know what I call it? I call it sour grapes. I remember the no-good, sorry-ass lokes you ignored me in favor of when I was young. You never had any man worth a fraction of Steve Reynolds look twice at you. Your problem is you don't want me to have what you never got."

Her mother moved as fast as a snake, and the sound of her hand striking flesh sounded like a shot. Carmel's head snapped back from the force of her mother's slap.

"You little ungrateful, disrespectful bitch," her mother hissed.

Carmel held her hand to her burning, painful cheek and backed away, her eyes wide and disbelieving, feeling as if she were thirteen all over again. Tears filled her eyes and she turned and fled.

She retreated to the sanctuary of her room, threw herself on her bed and looked up at the ceiling, the feeling of déjà vu strong. But no, this was worse. The unsaid and unspoken had come into open air. It had a penetrating, rotten odor. A rift had reopened between her and her mother that might never close all the way.

She'd never faced the resentment that she had of her mother. There were a lot of things she never faced. Her anger at her mother and the boyfriends that she paid attention to while Carmel felt her needs ignored. The anger that her mother never protected her . . . Carmel turned her face against the wall. No, there were things she still couldn't think about.

Chapter 19

"What I don't understand is why you don't look a
whole lot happier. You've been moping around all
afternoon," Jasmine said to Carmel. They sat cross-
legged in the middle of Carmel's bed with a growing
pile of foil candy wrappers from chocolate kisses
between them.

Carmel shrugged.

"Maybe I don't get the entire picture. Please correct me if I'm mistaken here." Jasmine popped
another chocolate kiss in her mouth and fell back
on the bed dramatically. "The successful, handsome,
no, make that fine, man that Carmel has been tripping over for weeks takes her out, then he takes her
to bed. Notwithstanding it's been four years since she
got any and it wouldn't take much—he subsequently
blew every neuron in her mind, not to mention her
body. Now, tell me, what's wrong with this picture?
You should be prancing around dancing."

"Melanie and Trey are going to be home from the

movies shortly. I probably should go get dinner on,"
Carmel said, not meeting Jasmine's eyes.

"Are you changing the subject? Without verifying
that I have the details straight? I think not."

"You got it about right. Especially that part about
my neurons being blown."

"So why are you sitting there looking like your dog
died?"

"I don't have a dog."

"Carmel!"

"Okay. It's just that . . . that it was too soon. We drank
too much. The mood was mellow, and we simply fell
into it. I don't think he would have normally . . . you
know, with a woman like me."

"With a woman like you? What's wrong with you?
The man has plenty of choices and if he didn't want
to throw down with you, I doubt that he would have."

"I was available and willing, Jasmine. What man—"

"The man wouldn't have taken you out to dinner.
He wouldn't have asked you out, period. In fact, he
wouldn't have spent any unnecessary time with you
one-on-one at all if taking you to bed weren't a possibility. Believe me, men don't work like that."

"Please. I've enjoyed friendships with plenty of men
and enjoy spending time with them."

"That friendship stuff between a man and a woman
is a figment of wishful imagination. I'm telling you,
no straight man is going to be up in your face unless
some thought of the possibility of jumping your bones
is there."

"I have no bones visible to jump," Carmel said, a
tinge of sarcasm in her voice.

"Are you still worrying about your weight?" Jasmine
looked into Carmel's face. "You are, aren't you?"

"Look at the women he's dated, at the woman he

married. They're tiny aerobicized specimens without an ounce of superfluous fat on them."

"And he wasn't with one of them last night, he was with you. Didn't seem like your weight slowed you two down any. I can look at you and tell he rocked and rolled you."

"Now you sound like my mother."

Jasmine grimaced while she digested that comment. "Your mama bringing that sweet potato pie for Sunday dinner like she usually does? I think about that pie all week," she said.

"I doubt if Mama will be around much any time soon. We had a fight yesterday."

"Over what?"

"She was upset that I stayed out late and came home looking like I'd just been bedded, to use her words."

"What concern is that of hers?"

"That's what I wanted to know. I think she's ticked because those days are far behind her."

"You're joking. You're not telling me she's jealous?" Jasmine said, a touch of incredulity in her voice.

"I don't know if that's the word I'd use, but my mother was quite a player in her day."

"Playing didn't seem to do much for her. You said she'd worked hard all her life as a nurse's aide and never married," Jasmine said.

"Yep. I reminded her that her men never did much for her." Carmel took a deep breath. "She slapped me. Hard. I haven't seen her since."

Jasmine sucked on a piece of chocolate, her eyes concerned. "So, who is going to watch your kids after school? You said you didn't trust them anymore on their own," she asked.

"You always do get to the heart of the problem,

don't you? I planned to talk to you about doing some kid-sitting," Carmel replied.

"I figured," Jasmine said. "Are you still going to be cooking those diet meals?"

"No. Everybody raised such hell. I'll fix something different for myself and cook for the family like I usually do."

"In that case, you know I'll be here for you," Jasmine said, looking relieved.

"I can't believe that you guzzle any fattening thing you want in vast amounts, never exercise and never gain an ounce."

"Fast metabolism. It runs in my family. Take solace that if we were in a famine in Africa, you'd live far longer than me."

Given the likelihood of famine in metro Atlanta, U.S.A., it was very poor solace, Carmel thought.

She wouldn't have to see Steve today. Monday was usually a day that Steve saw office patients, but today Carmel remembered he'd said he had a major reconstructive plastic surgery scheduled. Tuesday and Wednesday were the days he was regularly in surgery. She had a reprieve until Thursday, maybe longer if he was taking call for other doctors. Lenore was reliable. She'd show up and be on time, so Carmel wouldn't have to stay late.

"Did you hear what I said?" Marvin asked.

Carmel's head jerked up, her preoccupied reverie snapping like a twig. "Sorry, I was thinking about something."

"My pest of an ex-wife called and actually asked if she could come over for lunch. When I said no, she said she was coming over anyway. I asked her why did she bother to call then? She said—"

"You and your ex-wife spend a lot of time together for a couple of arch enemies," Carmel said. She thought of what Donna's sister Vicky had said about her husband having a heart attack and wondered if she should mention it to Marvin. No, it was none of her business. Best to stay out of it.

"Huh? Just because she comes over here at the drop of a hat doesn't mean we 'spend a lot of time together.' What do you mean by that statement anyhow?" Marvin demanded, a scowl on his face.

"Nothing but what I said."

"Her son does live here, you know."

"She comes over mostly when Steve is at the office, to talk to you."

Marvin snorted and shifted in his chair. "To torture me, you mean. He raised an eyebrow at her. "You don't like her coming over because she's such a bitch to you, eh?"

Carmel didn't reply, but her lips tightened.

"Don't feel bad, she's like that to almost everybody. She and Sienna did get on well. Two peas in a pod. They always had a lot to talk about, mainly about other folks, their latest beauty treatments and what was on sale at Neiman Marcus. You're worth the both of them put together and I'm not just talking about weight."

Carmel couldn't stop her eyes from filling at the jab. Right now, her nerves were stretched and frayed, especially in matters pertaining to her weight.

"I didn't mean to upset you," Marvin said, his sharp eyes not missing a thing. "Donna hates fat people. Always has and always will because it's her worst fear that it could happen to her. Her sister's fat and her mother was fat. That's what I was trying to say."

Carmel didn't quite trust herself yet to speak, so she remained silent.

"Her beauty is all she's ever had and she knows it. Sienna is the same. That's the only thing that gives them the edge to head the pack. If they were average-looking, they'd be average people with average lives," he continued.

"Like me, right?" Carmel asked, bitterness edging her voice.

Marvin craned his head around and stared at her. "There's nothing average about you," he said. "The better I know you, the more I see you're well-proportioned and womanly. And you are far prettier than Sienna or even Donna in her heyday."

Carmel sniffed.

Marvin handed her a tissue. "Is it that time of the month?" he asked, sympathy dripping from his voice.

The outrageous question sent her over the edge and she giggled as she wiped her eyes. "No, it's not that time of the month. That was the nicest thing anybody has said to me in a long time, that's all."

The look on Marvin's face broadcast his snort as well as any exclamation would have. "Well, it's true. I'd much rather have you as a daughter-in-law than that Sienna. She didn't know when to keep her mouth shut and when to say something like you do. She played all those stupid female games instead of going after what she wanted directly." He arched an eyebrow at her, and looked so much like Steve for a moment her breath caught. "Speaking of, I hear you and my son had a good time last weekend."

Oh Lord, Carmel thought. Did Steve tell his Dad that they . . . ?

"At least he said he did. You've looked somewhat distraught ever since you got in this morning. Regrets?"

Carmel choked, speechless, her once moist eyes

feeling like they were lined with sandpaper. The son of a bitch did tell him.

"No, he didn't tell me anything," Marvin said, apparently reading her mind. "I can tell you're upset about something, and every time I've mentioned my son's name you look like you're going to have a heart attack."

"If I have a heart attack, you're the one who's giving it to me," she said.

"That's another thing I like about you. Sweet, but got a spicy mouth on you. A hell of a combination."

Carmel rolled her eyes.

Marvin chuckled at her disgruntlement. "Any more of those tasty cinnamon rolls you made? I'd sure like another one and some fresh coffee."

"Sure." She got up and went to the kitchen. She'd have one or two herself. The hell with this diet stuff. It was making her miserable and she wasn't losing any weight anyway.

Chapter 20

Carmel headed out of the kitchen carrying a steaming hot cup of coffee for Marvin into the den. It was almost a week after the tryst with Steve, and Carmel had managed to stay out of his way. Lenore was supposed to come in early today so Carmel could get out of there well before Steve came home.

Friday afternoon and she was almost home free. She planned to take the weekend to think hard about her life and priorities. Something was going to have to change. She was sick of feeling dissatisfied, of feeling—

She bumped into a hard form, spilling hot coffee all over them both. Steve. Expletives came from them simultaneously, Steve's likely from the pain of hot coffee on nerve endings, hers more from sheer frustration.

"I'm sorry," Carmel said, dashing into the kitchen for paper towels to help clean him up.

"Wait a minute," he said. "It's all right. I planned

to take a shower anyway." He hesitated, a wicked light glinting in his eyes. "Want to join me?"

Carmel looked around wildly, flustered at his invitation and the thought that someone might have overheard him.

"No. No, I don't want to," she said, her voice a little too sharp.

"What's wrong, Carmel? Why have you been avoiding me?"

A too-long moment of silence came between them. "You think I'm avoiding you?" she parroted.

"I know it. What I don't know is why. I thought we were good together."

She looked down, mortified, confused. He took her hand and drew her to his study. "Come here. We need to talk."

"But your father—"

"Can wait. Come on." He grabbed her by the arm and propelled her into his study, firmly closing the door behind him. He leaned back against the desk and drew her close. "Now tell me what's going on."

What was going on was that she could barely breathe, much less talk, standing so close to him.

He pulled her closer. She could feel his body heat. "Carmel?" he asked, his voice a husky whisper.

"Nothing's going on. I've been busy, that's all."

He slowly drew her in his arms and tipped her face up. "I don't buy it. Tell me, Carmel. I don't like being shut out. I thought everything was wonderful between us last weekend, then you disappeared."

"It was wonderful. But . . ." Her voice trailed away and silence lengthened.

"But?" he prompted gently.

"It was too soon. I feel like I pushed you into something you may not have wanted to do."

"Do I seem like a man who does anything he doesn't want to do of that nature?"

"No, but—"

"No more buts," he said, and touched his lips to hers. The kiss was tender, full of affection, gently coaxing a response from her. It set Carmel's senses reeling and every defense she had unraveled.

His hands cupped her and pulled her close to him. She couldn't stop herself any more than she could stop breathing. Her arms wound themselves around his neck and her hips ground into his, mindlessly seeking fusion. His kiss deepened, tenderness transforming into hungry passion.

The mindless state that overcame Carmel at the hotel slipped over her now. She could no longer think, no longer care about logic and reason and caution. All she could do was feel and want this man, this one man . . . him only.

She heard a gasp behind her cushioned in layers of cotton, like a dream. Then sharply, peremptorily, the words as cutting as a knife, "My God Steven, what are you doing?" rang out in tones of disbelief laced with disgust. Donna.

Steve lifted his head, barely stifling a sigh. Carmel swung around slowly, still feeling mired in honey.

"What does it appear like I'm doing, Mom?"

Donna's upper lip curled. "It appears sickening. I thought I raised you with more self-respect. How could you relieve your base desires with a woman who has no respect for herself. Look at her! How could you lower yourself to—"

"Get out of my office," Steve ordered Donna. His voice was low and entirely reasonable.

"What did you say to me?"

"I told you to get out of my office."

"How dare you speak to me like that," Donna screeched.

Steve took Carmel's arm. "Come on. She's not leaving, so we will." He swept her past Donna toward the den where Marvin was sitting.

Marvin looked up from his book. "Dad, I'm taking Carmel away for a while," Steve said. "Mom came into my office and she really pissed me—"

Donna stormed in the room and pointed a finger at Carmel. "You unprofessional slut. I'm reporting you to the Board of Nursing. You don't deserve that license you say you have."

Marvin took off his glasses and frowned at Donna.

Carmel saw Steve's eyes narrow dangerously. "Apologize to Carmel and get out of this house," he said.

"I'm not saying anything to that fat pig. And you remember that I'm your mother."

"I don't care who you are. This is my house and you need to respect that fact. You're not welcome here until you apologize."

"Marvin! Are you going to allow him to talk to me like that?"

The look Marvin gave Steve looked suspiciously like one of pride. "Yep."

"Mom, go home. Spend some time with your husband. Vicky told me that he hadn't gone to work yet since his heart attack."

Marvin cocked his head and looked at Donna. "You gave Gene a heart attack?"

Carmel inched toward the door. Unlike Donna, she was more than ready to book. If that witch directed one more rude word to her, she was going to take off her shoe and crown her upside her head à la Jerry Springer.

Donna burst into tears. "Mumfph, mumfph, mumfph," she snorted unintelligibly.

"Steve, I've got to go," Carmel said. He nodded, but continued to watch his mother in fascination.

"I can't go home. He hates me. He wants me out of the house. He was on top of some woman when it happened, and, and—" Donna wailed.

Carmel hesitated. This was starting to get interesting.

Donna staggered to the couch, got a handful of tissues from the box on the end table and blew her nose noisily. "He was pumping some file clerk from his office on our bed when he had his heart attack. He's filing for divorce. And that's not the worst part. I signed a prenup!" she wailed again, bursting into a fresh fount of tears.

Steve pinched the bridge of his nose between his thumb and forefingers.

Marvin snorted. "So what does that got to do with you disrespecting Carmel? Steve means what he says, you'd better apologize."

The doorbell rang. "Let me get that," Carmel said, escaping from the room. Lord, Carmel thought. And she'd thought her mother was a trip.

The doorbell rang again, then again. "Hold on. I'm coming," Carmel called. She pulled open the door to confront Sienna's beautiful, petulant face. "You," Sienna said, managing to register scorn and dismissal in that single syllable. She swept past her toward the voices in the den.

"Ms. Lake, I'd wait a moment if I were you," Carmel started to say.

"Don't you just wish you were?" Sienna asked. "Don't bother yourself. I used to live here and I'm family." With those words Sienna turned her back to her and went on to the den. Carmel shrugged and followed her.

"Sienna!" Donna cried upon seeing her. "I didn't

get a chance to talk to Steve about your news." Sienna's glance flickered over her. "What's wrong with you?" But when Donna opened her mouth to tell her, Sienna turned her away and flung herself on Steve. He rocked, but lost his balance anyway and fell against the wall, hitting his head with a loud thunk. Carmel winced in sympathy.

"I couldn't wait a moment later, darling," Sienna cried, oblivious. "I had to tell you the wonderful news." She let two beats pass for obvious dramatic effect. "I'm pregnant!"

Steve's jaw dropped and he stared at Sienna in consternation. Donna beamed. Carmel met Marvin's eyes and jerked her head toward the door. I'm getting out of here, she telegraphed. Marvin nodded imperceptibly.

Carmel wheeled and grabbed her jacket and purse. When the front door closed behind her, she took a deep breath. What a freaking circus, she thought as she walked to her car.

Chapter 21

The house seemed too quiet when Carmel walked in. The kids must not be home from school yet. She took off her coat and threw it and her purse across the couch instead of hanging the coat in the closet. She always got on Melanie about that, she thought, but let them lie there anyway.

Carmel walked straight into the kitchen, and the next thing she knew she was standing in front of the open refrigerator, staring inside. Ham. She got out some Texas toast from the freezer and put it into the toaster oven while she carved off a thick chunk of ham. She stared impatiently at the browning bread. The toaster oven clicked off and she slathered the toast with mayonnaise and put two slices of American cheese and the chunk of ham between them.

She slapped the sandwich closed, then dug around in the back of the refrigerator for that two-liter bottle of cola she kept for Trey. She didn't bother to pour it into a glass. She wrapped the sandwich with a paper towel and sat on the couch in front of the TV. She reached for the remote. Jerry Springer. Totally appropriate fare for her present mood.

It took about four bites to down that sandwich, and she headed to the kitchen to make another one. She finished the second sandwich and sat unseeing in front of the brawling, beeping folks on the television. She wished there was something sweet in the kitchen except Fig Newtons.

She rose again and rummaged through the cabinets. There. Trey's Breakfast Sugar Bombs. She got out a regular bowl and put it back. Nope, that wouldn't do at all. She got out a mixing bowl, filled it with Sugar Bombs and topped it off with a quart or so of milk.

The bowl was empty by the time Springer was over. She felt more than a touch sick, but she got up to clean up all traces of her binge before Melanie or Jasmine arrived. She was full up, numbed out. She didn't have to think about Donna's insults, or Steve's kisses, or the estrangement from her mother, or Sienna being pregnant by Steve. She closed her eyes in pain momentarily. Then she swiped the mixing bowl with a dishtowel and put it back where it belonged. She got back to the living room in time to hear the Oprah theme. Nope, she didn't have to think about a thing.

Jasmine leaned back in her chair and sighed with contentment. "That was more than worth the grocery trip I had to make. Great meal, Carmel."

"Thanks," she said, sitting down at the table with her second helping of strawberry shortcake. She'd gone back to her former way of cooking with a vengeance. Beef brisket, fresh string beans cooked with salt pork until they were utterly limp and begging for mercy, potatoes mashed with real butter and cream, and strawberry shortcake for dessert. Not an undercooked vegetable, whole grain or lettuce leaf in sight. The strawberries were fresh though, Carmel thought. They should count as a vegetable.

To Carmel's relief, Melanie cleaned her plate and went back for seconds. Apparently the diet was history and Carmel was glad of it.

Jasmine speared a last strawberry and groaned in contentment, then pushed back her chair. "I'm going to start the dishes, do you want anything else from the kitchen?" she asked Carmel.

"Some more shortcake." Carmel handed her the bowl.

The doorbell rang, and she heard Trey, who'd already excused himself from the table, run down the stairs to get it.

"Mom, somebody's here to see you," he called a few seconds later.

Carmel frowned, unable to imagine who it could be. When she reached the living room she bit her lip to stifle a gasp. Steve stood there looking concerned and unhappy and so good.

"Hello, Steve. I'm surprised to see you."

"I needed to talk to you.

Carmel nodded. "Would you like dinner? I have strawberry shortcake."

He shook his head a touch impatiently.

"Coffee? Would you like coffee?" she asked.

"No. I just want to talk to you. In private, preferably."

The only place more private than they were now was her bedroom, and she wasn't about to take him there. She grabbed the remote and turned on the

TV to drown out any echo of their voices. "This is as private as it gets. Won't you have a seat?"

He sat on the sofa and Carmel moved to the far side of it, almost hugging the arm. He moved closer, too close. "I'm not going to try to talk over the television."

He took her hand, and Carmel bit her lip again, her feelings swirling and confused inside. "First I've got to apologize for my mother. How she treated you was totally uncalled for."

Carmel shrugged. "I'm starting to get used to it."

Steve's lips thinned. "Mom wants to move in."

"I'll start looking for another nurse to fill my shifts," Carmel said without hesitation.

Steve ran his hand over his hair, "I'm not going to let her move in. She'd turn the place upside down and drive Marvin and me crazy. I just wanted to apologize for her. Her behavior toward you has been . . . unforgivable. It will stop. I let her know very clearly that I won't tolerate it in my house."

"I wonder why she's so hostile to me?"

"I don't know. She's not nice to most people though. But she and Sienna always hit it off."

Carmel looked at him sideways through her lashes. "Did you and Sienna get everything worked out?"

"I doubt that there is anything to work out. I don't see how it could be mine."

"So you're saying that there's not a possibility that you could be the cause of Sienna's pregnancy?"

He hesitated, a fraction of a moment too long.

"There is the possibility that Sienna's child could be yours?" Carmel almost whispered.

Steve shook his head. "It doesn't make sense that she could be four months pregnant and is just speaking up now."

She stood. "It sounds as if you have a responsibility.

I've never thought much about men who didn't own up to their actions or their children. I have had intimate acquaintances with the type. It happened to me twice."

"It was a stupid thing to do," he said, looking pained. "Sienna had asked me to come over to her place late one evening about four months ago. She said it was an emergency. When I got there she was in tears, nearly hysterical. She said her job was in danger because she'd refused her boss's sexual advances. She begged for my advice. I'd never seen her so vulnerable before. It was a more appealing side of her than I'd seen for years. I had a few drinks. It had been a long time since I'd . . . and one thing led to another. I regretted it as soon as it was over. I realized the whole thing was a ploy to get me over there and the sex was simply leverage over me. I felt like a fool."

Carmel shook her head slowly, sadly. "I'm sorry, but what's done is done. You have a responsibility."

He cupped her chin up and looked in her face. He appeared to be drinking her in and all of the sudden Carmel felt dizzy. "There has to be a way," he whispered. "You can't pull away from this."

Jasmine entered, and stopped abruptly, surprise on her face. Carmel moved away from Steve. "Jasmine, have you met Dr. Steve Reynolds?"

"Just on the phone," she said.

He smiled at Jasmine, that sideways smile that Carmel found so endearing. "It's good to finally meet you."

"I need to talk to you for a moment," Jasmine said to Carmel.

"What's going on?"

Jasmine darted a glance at Steve and drew Carmel

toward the kitchen. "It'll just take a second. I'll bring her right back."

The kitchen door shut behind them. "So what was so important?" Carmel asked.

"It's Melanie. I went upstairs to your bathroom because Trey was in the bathroom downstairs. Melanie was in the bathroom upstairs."

Carmel frowned. "You pulled me away from Steve to tell me you couldn't get into the bathroom? Tell one of the kids to hurry up and get out."

"No, I didn't pull you away from that man to tell you that. I heard Melanie throwing up in the bathroom. She sounded really sick, so I opened the door to check on her. She was standing over the toilet with her finger down her throat. When I questioned her she was sullen and evasive."

Carmel ran a hand through her hair. "Are you sure? She was really trying to make herself throw up? She could have been just sick to her stomach and wanting to get it out."

Jasmine gave her an exasperated look. "Carmel, I know what I'm talking about. I wouldn't have dragged you in here if I didn't think it was serious."

Carmel bit her lip in worry. "I'm going to have to talk to her. What else is going to happen? I can't believe all this. I feel like I'm on the verge of . . ."

"Verge of what?"

"I'd say homicide, but I'll settle for a nervous breakdown and a month in a plush sanitarium."

Jasmine shook her head. "Go take care of that man, then come and take care of the home front. You can handle it."

Chapter 22

Carmel walked slowly from the kitchen to the living room with what Jasmine revealed about Melanie lying heavily on her mind. Steve paced impatiently with his head down, seemingly deep in thought.

"Steve," she said. He swung around and met her eyes. "Let's take a ride. I need some fresh air," she said.

She had to get out of this house. She felt as if she were suffocating, the walls closing in on her. What she heard about Melanie made her feel upset, fearful for her daughter, and most of all, guilty. Before she'd gone off on a tangent with her own dieting struggle, Melanie had been an athletic thirteen-year-old who gloried in the agility and strength of her body. Now she was sullen and unhappy with herself.

Carmel could almost see her child's self-esteem and well-being draining out of her. She'd been so relieved when Melanie apparently quit her diet and her obsession with becoming thin. But with self-induced vomiting, preoccupation had escalated into illness.

"Carmel?" Steve asked, startling her out of her reverie. He held out her jacket.

"Hold on," she said. "I've got to tell Jasmine we're leaving."

She stuck her head in the kitchen door. "I'm going for a ride with Steve. We'll be back shortly. Do you mind?" Jasmine put a plate in the dishwasher and waved her on.

When she returned, Steve put his hand at the small of her back, following her out the door. His hand radiated warmth and the memory of how good it felt touching her body aroused her even more. She shook her head, disgusted with herself that she could be thinking about lovemaking with so many other worries swirling in her head.

Steve opened the car door for her and she slipped into the leather seat. He turned the ignition and the motor came to life with a purr. "Where do you want to go?"

"It doesn't matter. I just need to get away from here for a while."

He pulled away from the curb. "Did Jasmine give you bad news?" he asked.

"Yes. Yes, she did." Carmel leaned back in her seat and closed her eyes. She didn't want to volunteer more, and even though she knew it was probably a faint hope, she prayed he wouldn't ask.

A space of silence lengthened. She started when she felt his hand clasp hers.

"I'm sorry," he said. "I thought we'd go and get a cup of coffee. I know a little place that's cozy and intimate. We can talk and they have great pie if you want some."

"Sounds good," Carmel murmured. It was testimony to the level of her inner agitation that the thought of pie made her feel vaguely nauseated. Or maybe it was the three helpings of strawberry short-cake.

The restaurant was casual, but dark and intimate. Exotic wall hangings and deep jewel colors gave it a Middle Eastern atmosphere. Carmel perused the menu. It offered several dozen different types of coffee. Her eyes skittered from the desserts.

"What can I get you?" the waitress asked.

"Whatever you're having is fine," Carmel said.

He ordered, and a minute later, steaming cups of coffee were placed in front of them. She took a sip. The coffee was good, but extremely full-bodied and strong. She might not sleep for a week after finishing this cup.

"It's an Ethiopian blend," Steve said.

"I like it."

"Good." He met her eyes. He looked serious and a touch sad. "Funny how we're just getting started and all of a sudden everything slips out of control."

Carmel nodded. "Jasmine told me she saw Melanie sticking a finger down her throat so she'd throw up. Melanie had eaten dinner, the first decent meal she's eaten in a while. She's been dieting."

"That could be serious."

"I know. I'm going to take care of it right away."

"I've never understood this obsession women have with dieting."

Carmel's eyes were solemn. "You don't understand how important beauty is to a woman in this society."

"No, what I don't understand is what dieting has to do with beauty."

Steve picked up her hand and his fingertips caressed hers. Their fingers entwined, fingertips against finger-tips, sensual and slow. The simple touch sent electricity sizzling through Carmel. Flashbacks of their night together flickered through her mind like a slide show. She looked into his eyes and knew he was remembering the same.

She wanted him. Shoving her worries firmly out of her mind, her tongue flickered out and she moistened her lips, feeling answering moisture . . . elsewhere.

"Let's get out of here," Steve whispered, his voice husky.

She got up out of the chair wordlessly. Their fingers touched, tangled and they almost ran to the car. She wasn't surprised when they pulled up to the hotel. He met her eyes, and her answering assent was plain. The valet parked the car, and with one pass of Steve's credit card, the magnetic key card was in hand.

Then they were in the room. He turned her to him and slipped her jacket off her shoulders. His followed and he gathered her into his arms.

Yes, she thought as his head lowered and his lips touched hers. Yes. They devoured each other, their passion growing.

She pulled his shirt out and ran her fingertips over the smooth skin of his back. He raised his head, his eyes darker than Ethiopian coffee, black with passion. Stepping back, he unbuttoned the first button of her long cotton and lace cream tunic. Carmel took a deep breath and closed her eyes as his hands worked their way down.

He started to slip the top off her shoulders and her eyes flew open. Ohmigod, that roll of fat at her midriff would be exposed.

She touched his hands, stilling them, and reached for his shirt buttons, unbuttoning them slowly. His hands reached through her open top to cup her breasts through her bra, his thumbs slowly rotating over her nipples. She couldn't stop the little moan that escaped her lips. He started to ease her blouse off again. She stepped back, fear overcoming her desire.

"What's wrong?" he said.

"Nothing's wrong."

Carmel walked away to the wall and flicked off the overhead light. Three lamps were on in the room.

"Carmel?"

She turned off the desk light and the bedside lamp closest to her. She started to the other side of the bed and he blocked her, pulling her back into him, his head lowering for another soul-melting kiss. She felt his hardness grind into her and thought her knees would give way. He reached behind and unclasped her bra, sliding his hands under it, then pulling it up and exposing her breasts. He set a trail of kisses down her neck, over her collarbone, to her nipple, his tongue teasing one into a hard peak, then another.

Molten lava. That's what it felt like, erupting from her core, flowing. She wanted him so badly; she wanted him inside her. Her hands were at his belt buckle, feverishly unloosening. They fell together on the bed.

She twisted to reach the lamp. "Please leave it on," Steve said. "I want to see you."

She froze, the heat ebbing out of her. He pulled her back on the bed gently, and sat astride her on his knees, straddling her hips. He leaned into her for another kiss, tender, coaxing. His hands caressed her shoulders, sliding the unbuttoned top down.

He unzipped her jeans and tugged them down over her hips. Her hips!

"I really want to turn out the light," she said.

"All right." He reached over and turned it off and Carmel sighed with relief as blessed darkness fell over them like a blanket. She reached up and entwined her arms around his neck, reveling in the feel of his tongue filling her mouth, the length of his body stretching out upon hers.

The onerous clothing that came between them fell away. Steve tore the foil packet and she reached for it, sliding it slowly, teasingly over his silken rock hardness. He groaned in pleasure.

Passion built as they touched and tasted each other . . . and when he slid inside her, filling her up, she thought she'd faint from the bliss of it. But she rode with him stroke for stroke on the feverish journey . . . until they reached ecstasy together.

Chapter 23

After their lovemaking, Steve reached out and
turned the light back on. Carmel flinched against the
light and drew the covers up to her chin.

He turned on his side and propped himself up on
his elbow. Reaching out, he trailed a finger lazily over
her cheek.

"Why don't you want the lights on? Don't you realize we men are visual creatures?"

She almost shuddered. That was exactly why she
didn't want the light on. How was she supposed to get
out of the bed and into her clothes? She wished he'd
left the light out. She wished she'd bounded out of
bed right afterwards, grabbed her clothes and made
for the bathroom, instead of lying there and basking
in the afterglow. Damn.

He was drawing the covers down. They'd almost
reached her midriff before she realized. She grasped
them in alarm. "No!" she cried.

He stopped immediately, his eyebrows raised. "All right."

He drew her to him again, the covers between them. Carmel felt his renewed arousal.

"Little Stevie seems to still want to play," he murmured.

Carmel couldn't help the giggle that erupted. "I'm more than willing to play with little Stevie anytime he wants."

Steve grinned and rolled on his back. "You on top?"

A chill passed through her. She loved on top, but . . . She started to sit up, planning to reach for the lamp.

"Why don't you leave the light on," he said.

No way.

She fell back against the bed.

Steve propped himself on his elbow and studied her, unconcerned in his nakedness.

"Why don't you want me to see you. By now don't you realize that I think you're beautiful?"

"How could you?" The words burst forth with an anguish Carmel hardly knew existed within her. "I'm fat!"

Steve looked taken aback. "You're certainly not skinny, but I thought I made it clear that I like the way you look. In fact, I think I've shown extreme enthusiasm for your body."

He grinned at her, but Carmel couldn't allow the mood to lighten. She was upset and she was mortified at what she'd blurted out. There were some things a woman should keep to herself.

"I'm going to get dressed," she announced. With as much dignity as she could muster, she stood up with the bedding still wrapped around her. She moved toward her discarded clothes. Then she almost tripped as the bedding held her. A corner was still caught under the mattress. She tugged, and tugged again.

"Need some help?" he asked, obviously trying to suppress a grin.

"No." She gave the covers a savage tug and finally she was free. Gathering her clothes, she lifted her chin and she marched toward the bathroom. It didn't improve her mood when she thought she heard Steve mutter, "Women!" under his breath.

Jasmine looked exasperated when Carmel walked into the door. "I thought you were going for a ride and be back in a few minutes, but you were gone for hours. Keith called, his wife is at one of her club meetings and he wanted me to meet him."

"Sorry," Carmel said.

Carmel hung up her jacket and joined Jasmine in front of the television.

"The kids are in bed?"

"Trey is. Melanie is up in her room, reading I think."

"I really appreciate you watching them tonight, and helping me out as much as you have."

"No problem, I got a lot of meals you've fed me to make up for." Jasmine looked at her closely. "You seem upset," she said.

"That news you gave me about Melanie shook me. I feel guilty, I suppose."

"I don't see why. A lot of girls that age have problems with their body image. The pressure to look a certain way can be tremendous."

"You've always been thin, haven't you?" Carmel asked, wondering how Jasmine understood so well.

"Being thin isn't the end all and be all of everything. In junior high and high school I was flat-chested and undeveloped *and* had skinny legs. Hell, I still got no breasts to speak of. But the size bra you were sprouting into was a big deal back then. I used to hate getting undressed for gym and showers. The other girls would look at me like I was pitiful. I couldn't wait until I could get a job and save up money to have my breasts done."

"You never got them done, did you?" Carmel asked, eyeing Jasmine's admittedly flat chest.

"Nope. I realized that a body is just a body and mine was as good as anyone else's. Any man I got that wanted me just for my boobs, well he wasn't worth the expense of plastic surgery, not to mention the pain."

Carmel thought about this a moment, surprised that Jasmine had had such significant insecurities in her past. She'd always thought of Jasmine as so confident about her body and her looks.

"I really screwed up tonight with Steve," Carmel said.

"What happened?"

Carmel sat on the couch and tucked her legs underneath her. "We went to a hotel."

Jasmine's eyebrows shot up. "A quickie? That doesn't sound like you."

"That's because you aren't tall, dark, fine and male."

"True enough. So how did you mess up?"

Carmel shifted, a little uncomfortable. "He wanted the light on. I just couldn't deal with it."

"Oh, I see," Jasmine said. "But he obviously knows what you look like by now and he must like it, so why the trip?"

"I don't know. It's hard to accept. I can hardly credit that a man like that wants me, fat and all. You see the type of woman he's been with. If he liked big women, why wasn't he with them before?"

"Maybe he never met one he liked."

"Believe me, there's plenty of us."

"Carmel, I hate to say this, but I'm going to lay it out. He's with you; he obviously cares. But nothing is going to lose him faster than you showing that you don't care for yourself. You need to make peace with yourself and accept who you are. Then maybe you can help your daughter also."

"Funny, that's what Mama said."

"Have you considered the tiny possibility that we both may be right?"

Carmel rubbed her eyes and sighed. "I know you're right. The problem is I can't figure out where to begin."

"Why don't you start with Melanie? It looks like you're both going through much the same thing. It's always easier to figure out how to help somebody else."

"Maybe I should make an appointment with a counselor for her."

"I wouldn't slough this problem off to the professionals. If you think counseling is in order, fine, but I think you need to be right in there with her all the way. It started with you and I think this can end with you."

A look of pain crossed Carmel's face, but she only nodded. Jasmine was right. She needed to figure out how to deal with this, at least to start with.

It was a typical Saturday morning. The kids sat in the family room watching television. Carmel struggled up the basement stairs with laundry. Halfway up she heard the doorbell ring.

"Grandma!" she heard Trey cry out. Great. She didn't feel up to dealing with her mother with everything that had happened.

She carried the laundry basket up and laid it beside Melanie. "Take care of these clothes, please."

She turned to her mother. Mama's arms were crossed over her chest and her eyes were cold, hard chips of black agate. Carmel bit back a sigh. One thing about Mama, she was predictable. She always knew she was right and she was the type to hold a grudge. Carmel hated to do it, but there was only one way to get straight with Mama. "Want to come into the kitchen?" she asked her. "I just put on a pot of coffee."

Carmel poured two steaming cups of coffee and slid the cream and sugar over to her mother. "I'm sorry about what happened between us the other day."

"You should be."

Carmel bit her lip. She'd just eaten breakfast, but suddenly she felt like having something else. Maybe another piece of toast?

"So what's been going on around here?" Mama asked.

"Nothing, just more of the same."

"Melanie still on that diet?"

"No, she quit it," Carmel said. And started something worse, she thought. She'd been checking the kids' upstairs bathroom closely and could detect the faint foul smell of vomit.

"I'm glad to hear that." Mama shot her a glance. "And how is your diet doing?"

"It's not." Thankfully, Mama didn't say I told you so. "Do you want some breakfast, some toast?"

"You got any rolls or doughnuts?"

"Uh-uh." She wasn't that far gone yet to have that sort of stuff in the house again, Carmel thought.

"Okay, I'll have some toast. Plenty of butter."

"I'm still very worried about Melanie. Much more than I'd been."

"Why is that?"

"Jasmine saw her making herself throw up after dinner. And when I check their bathroom I can see some traces under the rim of the bowl sometimes."

Mama set her cup of coffee down. "That sounds serious. At any age I'd be concerned but especially at thirteen."

"I know. I've made an appointment for us to go to a therapist for evaluation on Tuesday. I haven't talked to her about it though."

"Be sure and do so as soon as possible. That's not the type of thing you want to spring on her." Mama took a sip of coffee thoughtfully. "I was hoping you wouldn't have as much trouble with her as I had with you, but I see that's likely not going to be the case."

Carmel was buttering the toast and her butter knife slipped and tore the bread. "I don't see where you had that much trouble out of me. I stayed out of your life and your sight most of the time. That seemed to be what you wanted."

"If your daughter comes home and announces she's pregnant by God knows who at the age of fourteen, maybe you'll redefine your definition of trouble."

"I had no choice," Carmel said. She gave her mother the only piece of toast left from the four she'd prepared, and popped two more in the toaster.

"Say what? From what you told me you definitely weren't raped. From what I heard, nobody made you spread your legs but your own little self."

"You didn't seem to give a damn about what I did

or didn't do. My friends were my family. My boy-friends were my family."

"Whatever may be the case, at your age you need to start taking responsibility for how your life was and how your life is. Talking about how you had no choice. You always have a choice. All the choices are yours and nobody creates your reality but yourself." Mama looked around. "You have any more toast?"

"In a second."

Carmel folded her arms across her chest. She hated it more than anything when Mama was right. Unfortunately, as much as she didn't like to admit it, that was usually the case.

"I'm not saying I didn't make some mistakes back then," Mama continued.

Carmel's jaw dropped. Mama was admitting to mistakes?

"But that was back then, and everybody makes mistakes. Folks nowadays buy all that psychobabble about how every damn thing in their lives that they don't like was somebody else's fault, especially their parents. Those psychobabblers are feeding those fools what they want to hear in return for the money they spend. I don't care what your parents did to you or who they were. Unless you got some sort of chemical brain imbalance, who you are today and who you'll be tomorrow is your own creation."

The toast popped up and Mama got up and strolled over to the toaster and reached for the butter. "Yeah, I done you wrong, probably really wrong. Your daddy done you wrong when he walked away from you and those boys that got you pregnant and split did you and their babies wrong. Folks are going to continue to do whatever they want to do, right or wrong. I know I am. So suck it up girl, and get your life together. I didn't raise a whiner."

After this speech, Mama slapped the two pieces of thickly buttered toast together and returned to the table. "Give me a refill on that coffee, will you?" she asked.

Chapter 24

"Have you heard the phrase 'the party's over'?"

Carmel turned from the paychecks to stare at Jasmine. "What do you mean?"

"That box of paychecks you have in your hand? Those might be the last ones we can give out without going into red ink."

Carmel sank into a chair. "This isn't just Monday blues you're talking, is it? We always said we weren't going to do red ink or risk bankruptcy. Is it really that bad?"

Jasmine nodded and then rubbed her eyes. "Not only can we barely afford to pay the few people we have contracted to work on the few cases we have, we can't afford to pay ourselves."

"We have the Reynolds case."

"That's our last private-duty case and the only skilled one. We just closed the other private-duty home health aide case we had. The state and federal cases are barely profitable. Anyway, when the new regulations come into effect we're going to lose those too. The lease is coming up for renewal. I don't see how we can manage it."

"I know, Jas," Carmel said with a sigh. "We've been putting off having this conversation, but we both knew it was coming. We didn't do too bad. We've had our gravy days. You got money in the bank and I've got a paid off home."

"Not bad at all. Most small businesses in our situation would be looking at bankruptcy. I say we made out like bandits, girl."

Carmel grinned. "Maybe we'll do it again. With something else beside health care next time, please."

"Yes, we should do it again. This isn't a failure. We did it right. We started on a shoestring with no debt and everything we made we either put back into the business or into our pockets."

"Yep, we're models of the American entrepreneurial spirit."

Jasmine wiped a suspiciously wet eye. "Yep."

"So now it's over. What's next?"

"Myers has someone to take over our lease if we let it go by the first of the month. I've got other agencies on line to take our Medicaid and Medicare cases. And as long as you've got Reynolds, you've got a paycheck."

"So do you. We're in this together. I expect you to take your share of the profit."

Jasmine shook her head. "I don't need it. I've got money saved. I'll take my time looking for a job. Your situation is different. I know you sunk all your savings into that house and you've got far more expenses than me. I'm not even talking about grocery bills here. Lord knows how important it is you keep me fed."

"But—"

"No buts."

There was a short pause. "Thanks, Jas."

The smell of the food Mama had made still lingered in the air, but dinner had been over for a while. She could hear the TV in the living room. Everybody was probably in there. Carmel had gotten home later than usual Monday evening. She and Jasmine had talked more about the process of liquidating the business.

Even though they were concentrating on the positives of the situation, there was a touch of grief left over. They had so many dreams and hopes when they'd started up. They'd done okay, but still the closing of the business meant the closing of a significant chapter of both of their lives. Endings and new beginnings merging together. The question of what directions they were going to travel next hung in the air like a giant question mark.

But she was home now and she had other things to worry about, like her children, Melanie in particular. She had to deal with her bingeing and vomiting. It was a serious disorder, but with Melanie only thirteen and it just beginning, possibly she could reach her. She'd thought long and hard all weekend about it. She considered not only how Melanie was dealing with food, but also the stress puberty and hormones were putting on her body image and desire to be culturally attractive. Carmel also considered herself. The problems started with her, so the solution had to start with her. It was a family affair after all, although weight loss had never been all that important to her before now. She had a plan. She only hoped Melanie would agree to what she had in mind and hang with her. At least she had to try.

She made herself a cup of tea and went over in her mind one more time what she wanted to say to her daughter. Then Carmel made her way slowly to the living room. Mama was lying on the couch watching a sitcom. She sat up when she saw Carmel enter. "You were so quiet I didn't even hear you come in."

"Hi Mama. How's everything? The kids?"

"I'm doing fine. Melanie came in after school with a bag of groceries and closeted herself in her room. Came out and ate dinner, seconds on everything, then sprinted back up the stairs. You talk to her yet?"

"No. That's what I'm going to do right now."

"Good luck." Mama turned her attention back to the show.

Carmel knocked at Melanie's door. There was a rustling. After a long moment her daughter called out, "Come in."

Carmel's heart hurt a little. She missed the happiness that she used to see cross her daughter's face when she came home from work.

"I've been preoccupied and working long hours. I've been wanting to talk to you."

Shutters slammed down over her daughter's eyes.

"Jasmine and I are going to have to close the business."

Melanie looked surprised. This was obviously not what she expected to hear. "What happened, Mom? Are you upset?"

"I'm a little upset, but I was expecting it. It's been hard for over a year. The money wasn't coming in and there were a lot of changes and new regulations."

"I'm sorry." Melanie paused. "What are you going to do?"

"I'm not sure. I'm not worried. I've never had a problem getting a job. For the time being I'll keep working where I'm working."

"Okay. That seems all right."

"I've been preoccupied lately about the business

and lots of things. I've been more worried and upset than usual. Have you noticed?''

"Well yes,'' Melanie said hesitantly. "I thought it was your diet.''

"That's been another problem. I haven't been able to stay on my diet, and I haven't lost any weight.''

"I have. I lost three more pounds.''

"I'm starting to think it's not dieting I need to do to lose weight, but I need to change the way I think.''

"Change the way you think? Why?''

"I think the way I think makes me want to eat so much food that's not healthy for me. I think I'm trying to soothe myself from upset or anger, stuff like that. You ever feel that way?''

Melanie looked away. "I don't know,'' she said.

"Sometimes I eat a lot of sugary comfort food, maybe even enough to make me sick. Then I don't have to think about what's worrying me.''

"Yeah. I do that sometimes.'' Her eyes skittered away again. "But it's cool. I'm not letting what I eat make me fat.''

"That doesn't matter because you're not dealing with the real problem. It's like just getting new players for your soccer team without dealing with what the regular players are doing wrong. It's not really going to fix the problem.''

Carmel leaned back against the wall and crossed her legs on Melanie's bed facing her. "Throwing up isn't going to fix the problem either. Besides, it's gross. What if Dean knew you threw up?''

Melanie looked alarmed when Carmel said the last sentence. "Throwing up is gross, but it's working. I'm losing weight,'' she said. "And no way Dean is going to find out.''

Carmel was thankful she didn't try to deny it. "I

did. There's an odor you know. And it's loud and sounds disgusting."

Melanie bit her lip.

"But that's not the worst thing about it. Wait here a moment." Carmel got up and left the room. She returned a moment later with an armful of books. "I was doing some reading and I found out that you aren't the first person to try what you're doing. She flipped open a page and showed Melanie a picture. "Look at her."

"Ugh," Melanie said, grimacing when she saw the picture. "What happened to her?"

"The same thing that you're doing. She threw up almost everything she ate to stay slim. Look at her teeth all rotted away. And her hair looks like straw."

"What's that over her face?" Melanie asked.

"Sores. Malnutrition of certain essential nutrients and the effect of the stomach acid on her teeth cause them. That's not all either. She's pretty jacked up inside too. You like to read. I'd like you to look over these books when you get a chance."

"But that's just her. She obviously went over into the deep end with it," Melanie said.

"Not really. A lot of people do what you do and start the same way you did. So many it's classified as a disease and there's even a name for it."

"Really?"

"Bulimia. And what you and I both do, what I've been doing for a long time, there's a name for that too. Bingeing."

Melanie stared at her and stared down at the picture.

"I'm going to work on myself from the inside out instead of the other way around. I wondered if you wanted to join me. Here, I got this for you." Carmel handed Melanie a large bound book. The cover was illustrated with pink and green flowers and the pages were blank.

Melanie studied the book with interest. "So, what are you going to do?"

"First I'm going to get at the cause of why I want to eat sweets and comfort food like rice pudding when I'm not hungry. Why I want to eat until I'm full and uncomfortable and I have to stop or I'll be sick."

"How are you going to do that?"

"I'm going to stop and think about how I'm feeling and maybe talk about it or write about it. Then I'm going to decide what I really need besides food and try to get it or figure out how I can. I got me a book too. I'm going to do a lot of writing about it. Maybe we can get together every day for a while and support each other."

"I don't know if that's going to help you lose weight. What if you can't get what you need?"

"Well I'm at least going to take the first step of letting myself feel what I'm feeling and trying to figure out what it is I really need besides Snickers bars or Oreos. There's more, but that's a start. Are you with me?"

Melanie hesitated, and Carmel's heart dropped. Then she smiled, a small smile, but with excitement and hope behind it. "I'm with you Mom."

Chapter 25

It had taken forever for Friday to arrive. Carmel looked out the window yet another time. She had a long talk with Steve earlier in the week and they had made some decisions.

They'd talked about Sienna's pregnancy and decided to face it together. Carmel sighed. Everybody made mistakes. Lord knows she had. No matter what, the child would have Steve's full support and would know its father.

They'd also decided that this was the night she'd spend the night. She'd been waiting an eternity for tonight. A whole week of simmering hot looks, accidental touches and stolen kisses had raised her temperature to the boiling point. But her anticipation was based on more than the satisfaction she knew Steve would give her. They were coming out.

An overnight stay put their relationship in front of their families and gave them a sense of legitimacy.

She and Steve were *seeing each other*. Tonight would make it official. They were an item.

She missed the idea of spontaneous lovemaking and lazy weekend trysts, but she had family and Steve had obligations. He'd gotten another doctor to trade call this weekend and she'd prepared the kids and gotten Jasmine to stay over. With this new man, Jasmine was usually free weekends, thank goodness. She didn't know if she could have faced Mama with this request.

"When are you going home? You're not waiting for another nurse, are you? I thought you said I was finally rid of all those heifers. I don't expect you to stay the night," Marvin said as he came into the kitchen.

Carmel turned slowly. Obviously Steve had said nothing to his father about their plans. The best thing would be to approach the situation directly, like an adult.

"Steve expects me to stay the night," Carmel said.

"Ooooo-eeeee," Marvin hollered, shaking his cane. "I didn't know the boy had it in him. Don't hurt him now, he's my only son." Marvin left the kitchen cackling.

Carmel's face burned as she stared after him. Approaching him like an adult hadn't made a whole lot of difference. She should have guessed she was going to get ribbed unmercifully however she told him.

Marvin stuck his head back in the kitchen. "I meant what I said about not hurting him. That boy ain't handled a real woman in I don't know how long. I'm glad your CPR is up to date. You might give that boy a heart attack with all that hefty nookie you're going to put on him." Marvin guffawed again and pounded his cane on the floor.

Carmel lifted her chin and passed him with as much dignity as she could muster. She'd have to introduce that man to Mama. At this moment she couldn't think of two people who deserved each other more.

That night Carmel lay in Steve's arms, content and satiated, feeling like that was the only place she belonged, where she needed to be. The whisper of gray morning light peeked through the curtains. Five in the morning and the loving still hadn't stopped. As soon as Steve had gotten home, he'd grabbed a bite to eat and they'd gone to bed early, much to Marvin's extreme amusement. Their hunger for each other couldn't, wouldn't wait. They'd make love and fallen asleep in one another's arms for a space of time, only to wake and do it all over again.

"Sleepy?" Steve asked, touching her nose.

"Mmmmm."

"You seem more comfortable with yourself lately."

"Thanks. I've been working on it," Carmel said.

"I'm worried about Sienna."

Her eyes flew open and she stifled the impulse to sit up in bed. He'd made love to her all night and chose the crack of dawn to mention his ex-wife's name. Guess that made sense. He might not have gotten any at all if he'd mentioned Sienna earlier in the evening. "And?" Carmel asked.

He shifted a little in the bed. "I can't believe that she'd be able to sit on news of that magnitude for months. She doesn't look pregnant. Did you see what she had on when she came over that day to tell me she was going to have a baby?"

Carmel nodded, remembering the skintight slip dress Sienna wore when she'd come to the house. Her stomach had been as flat as a pancake. Her breasts too. "The woman has the figure of a snake."

"A snake?" Steve asked.

Oops. She must have said the words out loud. Catty, catty, she admonished herself. Pull those claws in. "What are you going to do?"

"She wants the entire enchilada. My name, my money, me. She says she wants us to be family again."

Carmel's insides turned to ice water and sloshed around.

"She's dreaming if she thinks she's going to get it from me," Steve continued, causing Carmel to feel a bit better. "But I worry about the child. It doesn't seem fair. My child deserves more." Steve pulled her to him, nestling them together like spoons.

Carmel agreed. The entire situation was a miserable one. She wanted to talk it out and make some sense of it all, but in a few minutes she heard Steve's breath fall into the deep regular rhythm of sleep. The morning light had turned pink before she followed him.

The late afternoon sun warmed the sky when Steve walked Carmel to her car the following afternoon.

"Thanks for lunch. It was wonderful," she said, turning to him.

She was pleasantly full and tired, with an unfamiliar wrung-out feeling that came after a night of loving. They ended up not getting out of bed until almost noon. They'd gone out for lunch and now their time together needed to end much too soon.

He touched her cheek and gave her a long, soulful kiss that she drank up like cool spring water. "Can I see you tomorrow?" he asked.

"Call me." Carmel smiled at him and slipped into the car. She waved to him as he watched her pull away. Steve Reynolds had a piece of her heart with him and he had to know it.

She glanced at her watch. She'd made an unbreakable appointment with Melanie, and she was looking forward to it.

They were going to talk about the food and body thing. It had been better for Carmel this week, although a little painful getting in touch with how she truly felt. When she realized that she was feeling something, anger for instance, she'd think about what she needed, say, to cuss somebody out. The problem was that she still wanted to stuff her face with Oreos or Ben and Jerry's Chunky Monkey ice cream, anything to take away the edge.

The act of bringing her motives and feelings to the forefront of her consciousness had helped her a little in not giving way to emotional eating. But it wasn't nearly enough. She'd thought of something, and she was anxious to hear what Melanie thought about it.

She used her key and found Jasmine lying on the couch, her nose in a book. She grinned when she saw Carmel.

"You have a good time?" Jasmine asked.

"Very good. How were the kids?"

"Pretty good. Quiet, anyway. I think this is the ideal age to baby-sit."

"It's a hell of an age to mother."

"Tell me about it. No, I take that back, don't. Melanie has asked about you three times. She said you had some sort of meeting with her."

"Where is she?"

"Up in her room. She's writing, I think."

"I'm going on upstairs to talk to her for a while."

Carmel made a cup of tea, laid down her things in her room and looked in on Trey, who was predictably immersed in a computer game.

She tapped on the door to Melanie's room and heard her daughter bound to the door to open it.

"Mom," Melanie said, her face alight with the love

and excitement to see her that Carmel remembered from . . . before she turned thirteen.

"Hi baby," she said, ruffling Melanie's braids. "I missed you."

"So did I." She thrust the diary in her hands. "Look at how many pages I filled up."

"How are you doing with your feelings? I noticed you haven't come to me for much support."

"Nope. I haven't needed to yet. I write or I call my girlfriend Denise on the phone and talk to her. But Mom . . ." Melanie's voice trailed off.

"What, baby?"

"I haven't lost any weight!"

Carmel sighed. "Neither have I. But becoming aware of our feelings is just the first step." She sat on the bed and Melanie stretched out beside her. "I read in a book that we have to be able to work through the pain of what we feel and set limits for ourselves."

"Limits?"

"Yep. We can't go on eating whatever we want and not exercising and expect to lose any weight."

"So you think we should go on a diet anyway?"

"Not a diet. I was thinking of three balanced meals and a snack daily. With nothing in between."

"That doesn't seem too hard. Do I get dessert?"

"You can have dessert. You're a lot younger and more active than I am. I don't think I can handle the sugar. Once I get started, I always end up saying that I can't believe I ate the whole thing."

Melanie giggled.

"I'm only going to eat sugar very rarely on special occasions. And that's not all. I think you get plenty of exercise with your sports at school, but I think I'm going to have to exercise also to get healthier."

"Are you going to play sports?"

"No, I think I'll take a walk every morning before work and one on Saturday, too."

"I'll go with you," Melanie offered.

"That'll be good. So that's what I mean by limits. We can't go on doing whatever we want and expect to be healthy. It's like we can't say whatever we want to our friends and expect them to like us, or go to school or work whenever we please and do whatever we want to do there."

"But that's not a diet. Are we going to lose weight?"

"No, it's not a diet. It's a way of eating I can live with for the rest of my life. If I can't lose weight eating like that and exercising, I wasn't meant to lose weight."

"Wow, Mom. Before you said you *had* to lose weight."

"To put it the way Mama would, I don't *have* to do anything. Neither do you. We need to be proud of ourselves for who and what we are. What would you think of someone who didn't accept the color of your skin, or the way your hair is?"

Melanie rolled her eyes. "I'd go off on them."

"You wouldn't go and buy skin lighteners and change your hair? You wouldn't be upset because they thought that you were not as good as someone with light skin and straight hair?"

"Heck no. They'd better stay out of my face."

"That's how we need to feel about our size. If we are living healthy, exercising, eating well and not bingeing, our bodies are what they were meant to be. Just like the color of our skin. And folks need to accept it or stay the heck out of our faces."

"I know that's right."

"Amen," Carmel said fervently, starting to believe it within her heart for the first time.

Chapter 26

Carmel opened the door and Donna swept past her, ignoring her greeting and giving her a disdainful head-to-toe glance. "Marvin!" Donna called, her high heels tapping on the foyer floor.

Carmel followed her into the den, where Marvin folded the paper noisily upon seeing her. He let out the heavy sigh that Carmel was feeling. "What do you want now?"

"Sienna just called me and told me that Steve wasn't returning her calls. She was quite upset. With her delicate condition I think Steve should be more considerate."

Marvin shrugged and picked up his paper. "He's a grown man. He can do what he wants."

"He's got a responsibility to our grandchild. Sienna wants to plan her move back in here and he won't even talk to her about it."

"Sienna's not moving back in here, pregnant or not."

Donna frowned. "Why do you say that? It's the decent thing for him to do. She doesn't need to be alone right now."

Marvin gave Carmel a wicked grin and her heart sank. He was going to let the proverbial cat out of the bag. "It might get a little crowded in his bedroom, with Carmel fitting in there so nicely and all."

"What!" Donna nearly shrieked. "Don't tell me he's screwing that fat cow."

Oh no. Now *that* was enough. Carmel stood with her hands on her hips and her eyes narrowed. "You need to stop being so free with your insults, Mrs. Graham. Or you're going to soon regret that mouth of yours."

"I know that's right," Marvin chimed in. "Knock her down, Carmel. I don't mind."

"You wouldn't dare lay a hand on me. I'd have you in prison so fast—" she stopped and sniffed. "I suppose it's typical of your kind to jump in bed with a man who loves another woman, a woman who is going to have his child. I just don't know what to make of my son lowering himself with such a low-class unkempt slut." She shuddered.

Carmel couldn't help herself. Her hand pulled back of its own volition and flew upside Donna's cheek with a loud crack.

There was a naked moment of silence. Donna touched her cheek. Then she shrieked and launched herself at Carmel, her scrawny hands outstretched.

"No one slaps me in the face, you fat tub of stinking manure! I'll rip every strand of that weave out of your head!"

Carmel reeled back. *Weave?* she thought as she shoved Donna away, wincing as Donna took a few strands of her hair with her.

"Fight, fight. Oooo-eeee," she heard Marvin yell.

But she didn't even get a chance to turn her head toward him before Donna had come at her again.

"You fat, sickening greasy pig. I'll kill you!" Donna shrieked.

So she wanted a fight, did she? Carmel thought as she knocked Donna's outstretched claws away from her face. She supposed she could give her one. She and the girls she'd tangled with years ago had never gone in much for that scratching and hair-pulling stuff. Carmel pulled her fist back for a right hook.

Marvin yelled gleefully in the background as they knocked over lamps and fell over furniture, Donna soon in full retreat. Then Donna wheeled like a cornered skunk and picked up an end table and brandished it.

Carmel paused. That table looked sort of heavy and she didn't relish the idea of it hitting her. Donna pitched the table with the strength and accuracy of Atlanta Braves pitcher Tom Glavine. Carmel dodged.

Then she heard a thud and a short exclamation of pain, and she wheeled in time to see the table hit Marvin and Marvin hit the floor.

He writhed in pain. "Call 911," she hissed at Donna, who stood there staring at her ex-husband in frozen horror.

Steve paced the emergency room waiting room in front of Donna and Carmel, who stood in front of him like contrite schoolgirls. "You two were fighting?" he asked with disbelief for what must have been the tenth time.

"She attacked me viciously. I'm pressing charges," Donna said, looking somewhat bedraggled.

Steve rubbed his temple. "If anybody presses

charges, it needs to be Dad." He darted a glance at Carmel. "What do you have to say for yourself?"

Carmel studied her nails. "Not a thing," she said.

Steve gave a snort of disgust, sounding exactly like his father. A nurse stuck her head into the room. "Dr. Reynolds, your father is asking for you."

He strode out of the room. Carmel turned to leave also. "Don't think you're going to get away with this," Donna said.

Carmel shrugged and moved to put as much distance between her and Steve's mother as possible. The sick feeling of guilt she had at the pit of her stomach wasn't going away. She knew better than to be slugging it out with Donna like they were both in high school or worse. And worse, she'd been on the job. If she'd been a nurse working for herself, she'd have fired herself without a second thought.

At least Marvin would be okay. But he had been seriously injured; a broken hip was nothing to mess around with. He'd be in the hospital for a while, have to undergo a painful surgery and an even more painful recovery.

At that moment Carmel felt like diving headfirst into a bag of Snickers bars and remaining there for several days. She stayed with her feelings, letting them build up to a sharp knife of pain. Then they began to fade away.

She was understandably upset, angry, mortified and worried about Marvin. But she couldn't wait to tell Mama about the fight. Then she'd pull out her journal and do a little writing about her feelings. She'd sit down good and hungry to a good, healthy dinner and not stuff herself, just eat until she was satisfied. Remembering how it felt to knock Donna down, she couldn't help but smile. She'd wanted to do that for so long and, damn, it sure had felt good. Snickers bars couldn't hold a candle to that.

"I wish I'd had a video camera. You should have seen it. Carmel kicked Donna's skinny ass." Marvin grinned, pure glee crossing his face at the memory.

"Was it worth you landing in the hospital with a broken hip?" Steve asked, a dry tone in his voice.

"Sure was. That girl has a mean right hook. Pow, bam, and Donna hit the floor screeching." Then he caught himself and looked at Steve. "Not that she really hurt your mother," he said.

"Mother looked a little worse for the wear, but more mad than anything. She says she wants to press charges."

"You know she's going to say that."

"Dad . . . What does Mom have against Carmel? She liked Sienna and the other women I've dated just fine."

"Those other women were like her. They had the same shallow, sorry values. Carmel's more like her mother and her sister. You know how she feels about them."

"Ouch," Steve said.

"Right. Being big is a major factor. It's always been Donna's major fear. In her mind that's what makes her so much better than her mother and Vicky, the fact that she's maintained a trim shape. She loses that, she feels she loses everything."

Steve shook his head. "She lost you and now it seems she lost this other man she married. She has a lousy relationship with her family, people who I think are wonderful, and I know she's not very happy. What has being slim gotten her?"

Marvin pondered for a moment. "A whole lot of clothes," he finally said.

They sat together in companionable male silence for a while, watching the game on TV.

"How do you really feel about that girl?" asked Marvin.

Steve continued staring at the TV for a moment. "I don't really know. I want to be with her. I like her immensely and the sexual connection is hot. But I feel sort of confused."

"Does Carmel's size have anything to do with your confusion?"

Steve took an even longer time answering this question. "Maybe. I've always been with women everybody else considers beautiful. I can imagine what some of the people I associate with will think. It's something I have to work through. But I think I'm old enough to be with who I want, not who somebody else thinks I should be with."

Marvin nodded. "Good answer, boy," he said.

Chapter 27

There was a tap on the door of his hospital room. "Come in," Marvin said. He was a little lightheaded from the painkillers they'd pumped him up with, but it was a damn sight better than being in pain.

A large brown woman entered the room, holding a spray of pink and white gladiolas that were wider than she was. That made for a whole lot of flowers. "Dr. Marvin Reynolds?" she asked.

"That's me."

"These are from me and my daughter Carmel," she said, setting the flowers on a nightstand across from his bed.

He stared at the spray in horror for a moment. "There must have been a mistake. Those look like they belong on my casket. Did y'all think I died?" he asked with a snort.

"I suppose a simple thank you is too much to expect from an old geezer like you. Do you think those flow-

ers came for free? Even if you don't like them, it's
the thought that counts."

Marvin was taken aback at her spirited defense. He
decided to change the subject. "Er, thanks. Sit down
and introduce yourself. And FYI, I'm not that old."

"You look old enough. My name is Edna Matthews.
Like I said, I'm Carmel's mother. She's my only
child."

"I just have one child, too." He studied her. He
could see traces of Carmel in her features. Good bone
structure. "So that's where Carmel got her pretty
face."

"Your comments on how you think my face looks
are very unnecessary, thank you very much. But now
that you mention it, you have quite a handsome face
yourself. Good bone structure."

Marvin stared at her, nonplussed.

"Not used to strangers commenting about your
facial features, are you? Neither am I," the woman
said.

Marvin cleared his throat. "How's Carmel doing?
I doubt that Donna will press charges."

"She's welcome to do so if she thinks that'll help
her get over the sting of her butt-whipping."

Marvin grinned. "Carmel did whip her butt. You
should have seen them. Donna wailing and screeching
and scratching like some kind of schoolgirl, then Carmel would move in and POP! Donna would hit the
floor."

Edna beamed with pride. "That's my girl."

"Yeah, it'll be nice to get back home with her.
These hospital nurses aren't worth a damn."

"I doubt after that fight with that woman Carmel's
coming back. She said you don't need a nurse anyway,
you just needed company. You were wasting your
money."

"I want Carmel back," Marvin said, frowning.

"Carmel's going to get a real job where she doesn't have to defend herself. Shoot, but if you pay me that almost thirty dollars an hour you were paying the agency for Carmel, I'll come out and give you all the company you want."

Marvin gave her a look. "You're a real piece of work."

"Thanks. You, too."

Dinnertime was better than ever. Not just the food, but something about the atmosphere had changed, Carmel decided. She supposed she had a lot to do with it since she decided to stop dealing with food as an evilly seductive enemy and make it her ally.

Jasmine had eaten and run, murmuring something about driving to Macon. Trey had cleared the table and rushed for the TV. She and Melanie were in the kitchen finishing up the dishes. "Dinner was good, Mom. This is lots better than a diet."

"Sure is." Carmel had fixed their favorite meal of fried chicken and mashed potatoes. She used real butter, but lightened up on the cream, using skim milk instead.

She served more vegetables, more lightly cooked with less fat. And Melanie and Trey had agreed to have fruit for dessert all the time. Trey got enough junk outside of home and Melanie said she didn't need sweets. So far so good. The changes hadn't caused the outcry her previous one had or near the misery for Carmel. She and her family still enjoyed their roasts, pork chops, fried chicken and catfish. They were meat-and-potato folks and there was no changing that.

"You exercise this morning?" Melanie asked.

"Yes, but getting started sure was a struggle."

"Most things that are worth it are," Melanie said, sounding uncannily like Mama. "Dean told me he gave Alexis a kiss and I wrote about it and I even cried. Then I called Denise and we talked about how much we hated her. But I didn't eat anything until dinner."

"That's great, baby. See, we're getting through it."

Later that night, Carmel settled into bed and thought about the way things were going. She worried a touch about whether her growing comfort with her body was because of Steve's obvious interest in it. She reached over to her night table and picked up the magazine with the picture of Tyra Banks and sighed. Just because she was struggling to accept herself didn't mean that if her fairy godmother arrived and gave her Tyra's body that she would turn it down. She still couldn't handle being on top with the lights on, but she was working on it.

She smiled as she thought of how much she and Steve burned for each other. Then a frown creased her forehead. What if it just was about the sex? She'd been carried away by the new experiences and blown away by the realization that a man like that really wanted her. For the past five weeks her brain regarding Dr. Steve Reynolds resided somewhere between her legs.

He'd told her he wanted her, he'd told her she was beautiful, but he had whispered no words of love. And most significant and telling, he hadn't taken her out publicly. She knew he got lots of invitations to functions.

Before she met Steve, all the women he dated looked like cookie cutouts of all the other women successful black men generally had on their arms. They were usually light-skinned, usually long-haired and never fat. Those attributes almost seemed like a prerequisite to have and to hold a successful black man. *Sour grapes,* her other voice whispered. *That's a bunch of crap and you know it.*

Steve had never made a mention of appearing in public with her on his arm. Am I only good enough for sweaty, lustful interludes in the bedroom? Am I the fat slut to him that his mother says I am?

She closed her eyes in pain and got up out of bed shaking the thought away. Before she knew it, there she was, standing in front of the refrigerator.

She backed away and ran tap water in a cup. Two minutes in front of the microwave like a zombie. Then it beeped and she dropped a bag of herbal tea in the steaming water. She was going to try something first before she gave in to the cravings. She was going upstairs and she was going to ride through the pain instead of running away from it. She'd been running from pain all her life and where had it gotten her?

The pain was still there with her, stored in her ripply thighs and the rolls of fat at her tummy. The first step toward letting it go had to be to pass through it. She got back into the bed and set her tea on the bedside table. Curling up into a ball, she let the fear and anxiety rack her that maybe Steve didn't want her, didn't love her, couldn't love her . . . the way she loved him.

A little later she raised her head, her cheeks damp with the traces of her tears, and picked up the now lukewarm tea. She felt a little better. No, a lot better. It felt so good to share lovemaking with a man she wanted as much as she wanted him. Her body felt more alive and womanly than it had in years. How did that old song go? *If this is the way that you're using me, then go ahead baby, use me up.* She fell asleep with that song echoing endlessly over and over in her head.

"Keith was going to take me out to this charity function this weekend. If someone said anything to wifey, he was going to say I was a business colleague. Then he cancelled on me, said something came up," Jasmine said.

Carmel pursed her lips, wanting to tell Jasmine what she thought of Keith so badly that she could almost taste it.

"Do you want to go?" Jasmine asked.

"Not really. That man is always standing you up and letting you down. Why, Jas? Michael was so good to you."

Jasmine's eyes narrowed and Carmel stifled a sigh. She'd stepped over the line and she knew it. Jasmine was understandably sensitive about this "love of her life," as she put it. Not sensitive enough to kick him to the curb unfortunately.

"Speaking of men standing you up and letting you down, I notice you and the junior Dr. Reynolds have made few appearances other than in the bedroom and your favorite intimate restaurant."

"You're right. Folks who live in glass houses shouldn't throw stones."

She could almost see Jasmine's defensiveness deflating. "Sorry, it's just that I'm so crazy about him, you know?"

"I know," Carmel replied.

"I think we should go. Get dressed up. Get out of the house. We've been in a rut and our lives are changing. Don't you feel it?"

Carmel nodded. "Things are different and moving so fast I can hardly get a grasp on them."

"Then let's move with it. Let's go out."

"Okay, I'm with you." The idea did excite her. She hardly ever went out, much less to elegant functions like the benefit seemed to be. "I wonder what I should wear."

"Something new," Jasmine answered promptly. "You deserve a new outfit."

"I probably do. Celebrate my unemployment."

"Nope, to celebrate getting to kick that heifer's butt. If folks only knew, I'd bet they'd want to pin a medal on you."

A laugh gurgled up from Carmel's throat. "I can't lie. It did feel good."

Chapter 28

"Jesus, look at that," commented the doctor sitting next to Steve while they documented their rounds.

Steve looked in the direction the other doctor was pointing, and saw nothing out of the ordinary. Phillip Shroeder, a general surgeon, was doing his rounds with his wife, a nurse who'd worked with him for years and he'd recently married.

"Poor Phil, ever since he married that woman she's been blowing up until she almost looks like a Macy's float in a parade. What a slob. But now he's stuck with her. He looks miserable."

Steve snapped his chart shut and stood. "Yeah."

"What fox are you dating now?" the doctor asked.

Steve shrugged. "Nobody serious. I got to get back to the office. Later, man." He strode away feeling both irritated and guilty. Is that what his colleagues and friends would say about Carmel if they appeared as a couple? Could he deal with it?

He didn't really know and that made him feel rotten. He'd thought he was a bigger man than to let other people's opinions sway his personal choices. But he was also honest with himself, and he was finding his feelings all too human. He hated his ambivalence, but he didn't know what to do about it. He worried about Carmel picking up on his inner worries he'd barely admitted even to himself. She seemed so sensitive. He had no idea what she'd do, but he realized that it wouldn't be good.

He sighed and reached for his car keys. He really didn't want to think about it right now. But the look of scorn his friend gave their mutual colleague's wife wouldn't fade from his mind.

"I'd love to see you tonight, but I've got some things to finish up before next week," Steve said.

Carmel curled up on the bed, cradling the phone to her ear. She loved the sound of his voice, everything about him. He cared so much about his practice. She could see him staying up late in his office poring over medical journals.

"That's okay," she said. "Jasmine and I had talked about going out anyway." She'd have cancelled in a hot second to spend time with Steve, but why tell him that?

"Have a good time. Um, how about getting together for brunch tomorrow?"

"Wonderful. And Steve?"

"Let's have it at the place we first . . . got together."

"Mmmmmm, sounds good. I miss you."

"Me, too."

Carmel hung up with a warm glow suffusing her. She was getting to the point where she didn't know what she'd do without that man. He was so nice, so caring and so damn near perfect. *What's next?* that irritating voice in her head asked. *You think you'll be hearing wedding bells?* the voice asked with a sarcastic tinge.

Shut up! I'm just enjoying one day at a time with him.

One roll in the hay at a time is more like it.

Carmel got up off the bed, resolutely shutting the voice out of her head, and went to the closet. She pulled out a red dress and held the hanger close to her, smoothing out the fabric. She never wore red. It was red leather, no less, cut low in the front with a modest slit up the side, but enough for an expanse of brown leg to flash through, and a cinched-in waist. Black belt, black boots and a matching leather jacket rounded out the outfit. She didn't want to think about how much the ensemble set her back.

She'd looked at the price tag and hadn't even wanted to try it on, but Jasmine insisted. They both stared at her reflection when she came out of the fitting room. She'd been transfixed by the woman reflected: sexy, voluptuous, wholly desirable. Jasmine had insisted she buy it, and she couldn't put up much resistance. Now she owned an outfit worth a couple of car payments. She held the outfit up against her body. It was worth it. She'd wear it with Steve when he took her out to a function like the one she was attending with Jasmine, or maybe a play or a concert. She couldn't wait until he saw her in it.

"Come in," Marvin called. A wide grin crossed his face when he saw Edna coming in with what looked and smelled like a plate of home-cooked food. Then he caught himself and grimaced slightly, creasing his brow into a frown.

"I see you're glad to see me," Edna said.

Shoot, that woman didn't miss a thing. "What you

got there?" Marvin asked, sitting up straighter in bed and smoothing his sheets.

"Your son said you could finally eat real food. So I brought you some. I checked out the hospital cafeteria. I don't know what it is they serve here, but it's not food."

"I know that's right. Sit it down over there and wheel the table over to my bed."

Edna had the bedside table in front of him with the plate of steaming savory food on it in no time.

"Smells like summer," Marvin commented.

"I like to grill year round. Atlanta weather is fairly mild and it sure makes the neighbors jealous."

"I bet it does." Marvin's mouth watered as he eyed the slab of barbecued ribs, potato salad, green bean salad and sweet corn with a couple of flaky biscuits on the side.

Edna produced a thermos and filled his glass with sweet tea. Marvin sighed in contentment as he dug in. "Did you bring a plate?" he asked a few minutes later when he looked up again. "I don't like to eat alone."

"Seems like you're doing a pretty good job to me."

"Humph," Marvin replied, his mouth full of barbecue.

The door swung open and Donna entered the room with her high heels tapping. She grimaced when she saw Marvin's plate. "All that fat and cholesterol will be the death of you. I can't believe they'd serve that swill at a hospital."

Her gaze swept the room. "This place is a pigsty." She pointed to Edna. "When you get finished, the floor needs to be mopped. Bring me some coffee first though." She shrugged out of her jacket and threw it over a chair. "Excuse me. Shouldn't you be working?"

she said acidly to Edna. "Get up. I want to sit next to my husband."

"This woman must be Donna," Edna said to Marvin.

He nodded and sucked a rib bone. "I'd wait until you get down to the parking lot before you kick her ass, if that's what you have in mind."

"That woman isn't worth the exertion it would take. She's not too bright, is she? Whatever made you marry her?"

"I thought I loved her and spent a lot of time trying to convince her that she loved me, too. Spent a lot of time trying to measure up to what she wanted and make her happy, too. I didn't have enough sense to realize that's not the sort of woman you can ever be truly happy with or grow old with. I let a few sweet, straightforward women who could have really *loved* me get away because I thought they weren't good enough for me. Yep, I got regrets."

Edna reached over and patted his hand. "Don't feel bad. Most men never realize that much," she murmured.

Donna's mouth had dropped open and her facial expression was outraged. "How dare you . . ." she started to say, sputtering.

"Notice how she didn't speak first like a civilized person or ask how I'm feeling like you usually do when you visit somebody in the hospital."

Edna nodded. "She's too old to change. She should have gotten her butt-whippings when she was younger."

"I know that's right."

"Marvin! How dare you?" Donna said, still sputtering.

Edna shook her head. "And she still doesn't get it."

"Like you said, she's not too bright." He looked at Donna directly for the first time. "This is Carmel's mother, Edna Matthews."

Donna's face screwed up in disgust and she started to open her mouth. Marvin held up his hand. "If you don't want to be occupying an adjacent room, I'd think before I started to insult folks. That's what got your butt whipped the last time."

"I'm leaving," Donna said as she wheeled and marched out of the room.

Marvin stared after her a moment and bent down over his plate of food. "I don't know what to do with that woman. She gets on my last nerve, but that is my son's mother. The best thing I can say about her is that she was a halfway decent mother."

"I feel sorry for her. She must have a lot of pain inside to want to be that evil to other folks," Edna observed.

"It's all of her own making. She thinks if she can make folks as unhappy as she is that it'll make her feel better. Did I tell you how good this food is?"

"The only time you looked up from your plate is when your ex-wife came in, and then you did so only briefly."

"Well it's mighty good. Guess I'm going to have to take you to a restaurant or something to pay you back." Marvin cast a sideways glance at Edna. "What do you think of that?"

"As long as you're picking up the check, I think it sounds pretty good."

Marvin grinned at her.

"I met your son the other day. You look just like him when you do that," Edna murmured.

"You mean he looks like me. Get it straight, woman. I'm the chicken, he's the egg and I came first."

"Right." She reached on his bedside table for the remote and flipped the channels. "*X-Files* is on."

"You like the *X-Files*," Marvin breathed.

"I don't think I'd be turning it on if I didn't." She leaned back in her chair and directed her attention to the television.

Marvin stared at Edna, the beginning of adoration dawning in his eyes. What a woman, he thought. Barbecue, common sense and *X-Files*. Did it get any better?

Carmel liked where she and Jasmine had been seated. Near the back, where she could see everybody but they couldn't see her. She smoothed her hands on the front of her dress. They were clammy. Picking up the stem of her water glass, she'd taken a sip just as the musical ensemble near the front started to play.

"Nervous?" Jasmine asked.

"A little. It's been so long since I've been out to something like this." She smiled at a distinguished-looking older couple being seated at their table.

Jasmine patted her hand. "You'll get in the swing of things. The music is good."

"Do you notice everybody is a part of a couple?"

Jasmine looked around. "Not everybody." She waved a hand to a few women, singular and plural, dotted around the room. "Lots of divorcees around here."

"If there's lots they must mostly stay at home." Carmel smiled at the couple across the table again, who were looking at them with a small amount of interest. The table was too wide and the music too loud for pleasantries.

"Mostly. It's a man's world. Always has been."

The waiter stuck a plate in front of them. Carmel supposed it was one of those trendy salads. Five or six slivers of vegetables that seemed to be chosen for their color alone, artistically decorated on a white china plate.

She was hungry. She hoped the meal was more substantial than the salad. Glancing over at Jasmine, she noticed that her girlfriend was surveying the room, probably checking out the men.

"You want to come to the bathroom with me?" Jasmine asked suddenly.

"We haven't had to go to the bathroom together since junior high. What's up?" Carmel asked.

"Come on," Jasmine said, sounding frantic, bending over to pick up her bag. Carmel frowned. What was wrong with the girl? Did she happen to see Keith here or something like that? Carmel looked over in the direction Jasmine had been looking and froze. It seemed as if the music crashed to a halt, all conversation stilled and the very dust motes froze in the air. To the left, near the front, was Steve with Sienna beside him, laughing up in his face, her hand on his arm.

Chapter 29

Carmel took a sip of the wine the waiter had thankfully served. Emotions boiled within her. He said he had some things to finish up on the phone. He'd implied they were things that had to do with his work, or she'd assumed it. But he'd let it stand. He never mentioned he was taking Sienna out.

She felt herself tremble. At that moment, if the ground opened up and swallowed her she wouldn't care in the least. She was a stupid fool. Why didn't she see his lingering interest in his ex-wife? Why didn't she feel it? How could she have been so stupid to think he'd cared about her. She bent her head as she felt her eyes fill, and willed the tears not to drop.

"Was that your husband?" The patrician-looking older blonde woman touched her hand. She'd moved around the table and sat at the other side of Carmel. "My name is Helena. I couldn't help but notice the stricken look on your face when you looked over at that nice-looking black man with that woman."

"No . . . He's my boyfriend. Or I thought he was."

The woman sighed. "Men are such dogs," she said.

Carmel thought she heard a strangled chortle from Jasmine and shot her girlfriend a glance.

"I'll drink to that," Jasmine said, picking up her wineglass.

Helena nodded sagely. "I'd like to give seminars to young women on how to control the dog pen. Heaven knows I've got experience." She cast a long-suffering glance at her husband, and he frowned.

She leaned in closer to Carmel and Jasmine. "See that man I'm with? I've been married to him thirty years and I was the other woman, so I know. Pure D dog with a capital."

Jasmine laughed out loud and then sobered quickly, casting a guilty look at Carmel.

"If this is your boyfriend that's appearing here unbeknownst to you with this—what term do you use? Oh, yes, *hoochie-mama woman*, you must take action."

Carmel could feel Jasmine next to her trembling from the effort of not howling with laughter.

"What do you propose I do?" Carmel asked.

The man glowered at Helena. "Pay him no mind," she said. "He knows I'm right. You have children?"

Carmel nodded at first then shook her head, "Not by him."

"No matter. The thing is not to let him think he's gotten away with it. Like a dog, the whole point is for them to steal the bone and get away with it. They will only cower if caught and reprimanded. So never be afraid to create a scene. You need to make an impression. Dogs are simple and direct creatures. They understand three basic things best: force, food and sex. Do you understand what I'm saying?"

Carmel nodded, thoroughly bemused. She heard Jasmine guffawing in the background. Apparently, her girlfriend couldn't restrain her mirth.

"Regain your control! You are his master, excuse me, his mistress. March right over there and chastise him. Pay that other hoochie-mama no mind. Treat her as if she's beneath your concern." Helena leaned farther forward and whispered in Carmel's ear. "Women hate that."

Jasmine stopped laughing.

"Look at him." She waved a hand toward her husband. "I know what I'm talking about. I've kept him in line and on a short leash for years, and believe me it hasn't been easy."

The waiter moved forward with their plates.

"She's pregnant by him. She wants them back together. He tells me that he doesn't want that, but now that I see them together . . ." Carmel said to Helena.

Jasmine's eyebrows shot up at the confidence.

"All the more reason to stand up for your man. Getting pregnant is the lowest hoochie-mama ploy there is. Go on, make a scene. I'd throw the wine in his face. That always works well."

"Helena, your food is growing cold, and I'm sure these young ladies want to eat," the man said. She waved him silent again. "You could knock him upside the head with a plate, but overt violence in a public place tends to be less effective."

Carmel nodded, and Helena returned to the other side of the table to her husband and her cooling food.

Carmel looked down at her plate. There was a minuscule portion of some sort of fish, half a tiny potato, a parsley leaf and what looked like a raw asparagus stalk. There were some dots of carrot, pimento and mushroom here and there for color and artistic effect. She sighed heavily.

"Carmel?" Jasmine asked. "I know you're not thinking about doing what that crazy woman advised you to do."

"She had a point, Jas. The man virtually lied to me, but it goes deeper than that. I've sensed that while he's perfectly happy with me in his bed, having me on his arm in front of his friends is less than comfortable for him. Aren't I worth more than that, Jasmine? Aren't I worth a whole lot more?"

Jasmine pursed her lips. "Of course you're worth more than that, but I don't see how creating a scene will help things."

"But it'll help me. If I sit here and cower in the back and pray that he won't see me, that says one thing. If I march right up to him and throw a glass of wine in his face, that will say another."

"It'll say you lost your mind."

"Well, maybe that's a little extreme, although if we were married, I'd think not. But I'm strong. I'm a woman, and dammit, I'm not going to take it sitting down."

Jasmine looked thoroughly alarmed. Carmel started to rise.

"Go ahead. You won't regret it, I promise," Helena called from the other side of the table. "Think of the look on his face."

Carmel started to pick up the wine.

"Carmel!" Jasmine's voice was sharp.

She paid her no mind and glided to Steve's table. She touched his shoulder and he turned, astonishment and shame written on his face.

"Hello, Steve. Nice to see you. I thought you'd be home *finishing up.*" She could see his face flush even under his dark skin. A nice grape effect.

She wriggled her fingers at him. "I just wanted to drop by and let you know I'm here. I'll be leaving soon. I have some things I need to finish up myself."

She turned and started to glide away when she heard Sienna's voice ring out. "I didn't know who that was at first. I thought it was a fire truck with all that red."

She slowly turned back around. "What did you say?"

"You heard me."

"Oh yes, I did." She reached over Sienna and picked up the half-empty wineglass in front of her. "Pregnant women really shouldn't drink alcohol," she said as she emptied the glass over Sienna's bone-straight hair.

That done, she turned and glided swiftly away.

Jasmine met her before she got back to her seat and rudely dragged her out of the room before she got a chance to thank Helena.

"I can't believe it . . . have you lost your mind?" Jasmine said once they reached the parking lot. "You have, haven't you? That was totally out of character! You listened to that crazy woman. In front of all those people . . . I can't believe—" Jasmine sputtered on in that vein all the way to the car.

Jasmine shoved Carmel into the passenger seat and started the car. "I'm not taking you anywhere again."

"Did you see the look on her face?" Carmel asked.

"No, I saw the look of horror on everybody else's face that saw that fool woman throw wine on folks with no apparent rhyme, reason or motive."

"There was too a motive. The bitch called me a fire truck. I was provoked. And she didn't need to be drinking that wine anyway."

"Are you listening to me?" Jasmine pounded her

hand on the steering wheel. "What has gotten into you? I'm serious, you answer me."

"I suppose I have lost my mind a little. He led me to believe that he'd be home going over his medical journals but he took that . . . that bitch out to a function with him. Like she's good enough to be seen with him and I'm not! I should have knocked him upside the head with a plate."

"And I'd be bailing your silly self out of jail right now instead of considering dropping you off at a mental hospital."

"Don't worry so much. That woman was right. If I'd let him get away with it and slunk on home, I'd be feeling rotten right now and drowning my sorrow in a couple bags of Oreos."

"Now, you're just the laughingstock of Atlanta."

"I doubt that. Those folks don't know who I am. Sienna probably looks pretty silly." Carmel giggled at the thought. "I got his attention though, don't you think?"

"Yeah, you got that."

"I didn't want to go out with a whimper like I usually do."

"You gave it a bang, all right."

"Let's go get a decent meal and celebrate my new-found liberation. I adore that woman. I'd sure like to find out who she is and thank her."

"You have lost your mind, you really have."

"I have a taste for Mexican. How about you?"

Chapter 30

She let herself in the house. The light of the television set flickered in the dark living room. The sound was off. "Mama, I'm home," she whispered, hating to wake her.

A long body unwrapped itself from the sofa. Steve. Carmel's mouth dried in shock. "Your mother left when I came to wait for you. Where have you been? I've been debating whether to call the police."

Carmel shrugged out of her jacket and hung it up in the closet. "Jasmine and I went out to eat."

She swung to face him, suddenly furious. "You need to be answering the questions, not asking them."

"Sienna is talking about pressing charges. If this is a taste of what your behavior has been like, I can see why you've been fighting with my mother, which frankly, was pretty incomprehensible to me before your ridiculous behavior tonight."

"Since my behavior is so ridiculous to you, I suggest

you get to stepping out of my house. Where's Mama anyway?''

"Dad insisted on coming home from the hospital. Edna went home with him.''

The thought of Mama and Marvin together disconcerted her so much she momentarily forgot the budding argument between herself and Steve.

"Mama's with Marvin and nobody's called 911 yet?''

"No, they seem to have hit it off rather well.''

"Geez. I'd have thought they'd kill each other.''

"They may, if we are alive to see it and don't do each other in first.''

He was too close to her. She backed up against the wall. She felt hemmed in and . . . hot.

"You led me to believe that you'd be home poring over medical journals," she said.

"I never said that. I simply said I had something to finish up, as you reminded me so *succinctly.*" He reached out and touched her cheek. She supposed she should have slapped his hand away, but she couldn't.

"I see you had no problem taking your ex-wife out to a benefit. I guess I'm a little too much to be seen out in public with, hmmmm?''

"What are you talking about? I've taken you out.''

"Restaurants and games. Places where we'd be unlikely to run into your friends.''

"What about that barbecue?''

"Oh.'' She'd forgotten about that.

It was late, she'd had too much wine and he was standing far too close.

"Admit it, you were jealous," Steve said.

"If you had any sense you'd quit while you're ahead," she answered. "You're changing the subject. This is an issue between us, a big one.

"Mmmmm. I'm ahead? That's good to know.'' He

bent his head and his lips touched hers tenderly, searching. He pulled her close.

"Stop it. We need to talk," she said. She closed her eyes in defeat as she uttered the words. The very sound of her voice was husky with passion. What was it with this man that overcame every sensible defense she had? That made her want to make love with him beyond all bounds and reason?

"I need you. I want you, Carmel, only you."

Any inkling of resistance faded. Her response was as natural as breathing. His kiss deepened and grew hungrier. She turned and drew him up the stairs. *One for the road,* the voice whispered in her head with a wicked chuckle.

Afterward, he held her and soon his breath fell into the rhythm of sleep. Carmel rolled on her back and stared up at the darkness. They hadn't talked. He'd made love to her and assumed that it made everything all right.

Pain caught in Carmel's gut. She couldn't do it anymore. She was feeling more in control and stronger than she'd ever felt before. She was coming to terms with who and what she was, and best of all she felt she was bringing her daughter with her.

The events of the night had brought what had been nagging at her for a while into sharp focus. She was worth a whole lot more than what Steve Reynolds could offer her right now.

The fact that Steve Reynolds deemed her acceptable enough to have sex with wasn't enough. Every time they made love he took a little more of her. Every time she fell more in love with him until soon she knew she'd be grateful to lap up any little crumb he threw her.

He wasn't ready for prime time. He had issues. Significant ones about her that he wasn't facing. Maybe one day someone would love her wholly for exactly who she was. Until then . . . she wouldn't settle. No matter how much she wanted this man. No matter how much she loved him.

She had to be strong enough to let him go while she still could. If he was ever meant to be hers, he'd return, with the weight of all the baggage and ambivalence he was carrying off his back. She had to let him go, so that one day, maybe, she would have a chance of truly wholly having him. In the meantime she'd have her self-respect. She shook him gently. "Steve, wake up."

He was one of those people who could instantly cross the line from sleep to wakefulness. "What's going on?" he asked, not a trace of sleep in his voice.

"I need you to go."

"Why?"

She hesitated. "My children . . ."

"All right. But you realize that your children are going to have to get used to me spending the night here sometimes."

She didn't reply, but his comment dismissed the last remnants of her doubts. He'd said her children would have to get used to him spending the night, but he'd never mentioned they'd have to get used to him sharing their lives.

She leaned back against the headboard once he was in the bathroom. Why had she lied? Why had she not told him that it was over between them? It was late and she was tired. That was a good enough excuse for now. It would have to be. Right now, although she'd made the decision in her own mind, she couldn't face telling him good-bye.

* * *

It was almost ten in the morning and she hadn't heard a word from Mama. She was burning up with curiosity to find out what was up between Mama and Marvin. Bittersweet anticipation of dealing with Steve made her reluctant to call his house. She missed him already, but she felt strong and resolute.

"Mom, is breakfast ready?" Melanie asked. "I'm starving."

"A few minutes," she said. One thing about this way they were eating was that they woke up hungry. Before, she didn't care at all about breakfast, but now since she seldom ate anything after dinner, she woke famished. It was a pretty good feeling. She'd just slid the omelet on the plate when she heard Jasmine come in.

"Just in time for breakfast. We slept late this morning."

"Coffee," Jasmine croaked.

Carmel poured her a cup after looking in her face. They'd gotten in late, but not late enough to account for those dark rings under her eyes.

"Keith came over last night."

"That late? But you said he couldn't get away to take you to the dinner."

"I don't know. I take my good fortune as it's handed to me without a whole lot of questions."

"Nice for him," Carmel murmured.

"Don't you start. I came over this early because I have news. Big news."

"Come and tell it to me over breakfast." Jasmine followed her to the dining table where Melanie and Trey already waited.

They'd settled in and were enjoying the food before Carmel remembered. "What was your big news?"

"I'm moving to Macon."

Carmel froze in the act of reaching for the fruit salad. "Moving to Macon? Whatever for?"

She knew the answer. To be close to that no-good cheating husband Jasmine fancied herself in love with.

"Keith is going to hire me for his company."

"Is that wise?"

"Good salary, good benefits. What could be unwise about that?"

Carmel was silent, biting her lip.

"I'm going to miss you all terribly, but I'm not far away. You'll still be seeing a lot of me."

"We're going to miss you a lot, Jasmine. You promise you'll be back to see me?" Melanie asked.

Jasmine's face softened. "Sure. Better yet, I'd sure like for you to come down and help me to get things in order."

"I'm going to miss you, too," Trey said. "It's like you're our aunt or something. You've always been around."

"I am an honorary aunt, and I'll always be there for you guys. You folks are all the family I have."

Jasmine sniffed and clapped her hands. "Enough gloom and melancholy. Change is in the air and we're all moving and shaking. Melanie, you look great, lost some weight?"

Melanie beamed. "I don't know. Mom threw out the scale. But my clothes are looser."

"Threw out the scales?" Jasmine glanced at Carmel. "You go, girl. And Trey is back on track. You kicked your boys to the curb, huh?"

"That's right," Trey said. "I don't think they liked me that much anyway. I was cheating for them so they'd pass the tests, but it wasn't worth it. If I got caught . . ."

"This cheating is news to me," Carmel said.

"I talked it over with Steve," Trey said. "We decided what to do."

"Oh," Carmel said. Jasmine raised her eyebrows.

"I almost forgot," Melanie said, jumping out of her chair. "Dean and I were going to play racquetball today. Can I be excused, Mom?"

Carmel nodded and Melanie dashed off.

"I'm right in the middle of Quake, Mom." Carmel waved him on and Trey ran up the stairs to his computer.

She turned to Jasmine. "It isn't going to be the same without you at the table," she said.

"We need a change, Carmel. We aren't getting any younger and maybe it's time to break out of our comfortable little ruts. Maybe it's time you looked at some other adult besides me or your mama at the table," Jasmine said. "And maybe it's time I did, too." She stood up and started clearing the table. "You doing all right?" she continued. "You were so different last night. Sort of spaced out and weird."

"It was a turning point. Steve was waiting for me when I got home."

"Maybe making a scene wasn't such a bad idea after all. I bet he cleared that whole thing with Sienna up, didn't he?"

"No. We hardly talked about it. In fact, we hardly talked at all."

"Oh. So you guys did some hot-and-heavy making up."

"Sort of. We were hot-and-heavy all right, but he didn't seem to think he had a whole lot to make up for. I made a decision, Jas. I have to let him go."

Chapter 31

Jasmine drew in a breath. "Let these dishes lie. We need to go get ourselves another cup of coffee and talk."

A few minutes later they were seated on the couch, each holding a steaming cup. "Did I hear you right? You said you were going to break up with Steve when he took Sienna home after you threw a glass of wine in her face and he came here and waited for you?"

"It doesn't have anything to do with what happened last night. That was just a catalyst for something that's been bothering me awhile. My decision has a lot to do with my self-respect."

"You told me you didn't talk about why he was with Sienna. He might have had a perfectly good reason. I know you're not crazy enough to let some stupid misunderstanding come between you without at least attempting to clear it up."

"No. I realize I'm not living in some sort of romance novel. It's not a misunderstanding. It's facts. The reason Steve was with Sienna doesn't matter, but his ambivalence toward me does. I'm good enough for creeping around in the dark, but not taking out into the light."

"Has he told you that?"

"Not in so many words."

"Aha."

"Aha nothing. A woman can sense these things. Steve has a lot of social obligations. I know that's not the only society function or charity benefit he's been obligated to attend since we've been together. How many pictures had we seen of him with some fashionable-looking woman draped over his arm at some function? He's never asked me to one, not once. The only social thing he's asked me to was a down-home, family-and-old-friends barbecue. It definitely wasn't a society event."

"Maybe there's some other reason."

"What other reason, Jas?"

"Okay. But remember, a man doesn't get over the habits of a lifetime overnight. He might know what he likes, but it might also take him time to share it with the world."

"I've been working hard on myself. I'm trying to accept myself the way I am and help my daughter to accept herself also. How would it help me progress for me to keep loving a man who doesn't fully accept me?"

"Oh, Carmel. You love him, don't you? And you're not like me. I don't recall you ever saying you were in love with anyone."

Carmel looked away. "I love myself more."

There was a space of silence between them as Jasmine absorbed this.

"I'm happy to hear you say that. But I still think

you need to give him a chance, especially if you care that much."

"That I care so much is one reason to get out of Dodge while I still can. Something in me wants to lie down and invite him to wipe his feet on me. Something inside me would put up with anything just to be with him. I need to be strong enough now to take the pain and get it over with, because if I wait much later . . . maybe I couldn't endure letting him go for whatever reason."

"If people didn't take a chance and jump in, I don't see how there would be any love in the world. There's always the risk of pain," Jasmine said.

"Then there's the certainty of it. He has old baggage to take care of. This situation with Sienna is still hanging in the air. And for him to have slept with her . . . well, there had to be some old feeling left."

Jasmine snorted at that. "Feelings down there don't have to have a thing to do with the head or the heart. You know that. You're making a mistake."

"I'm not. I'm too tangled up when I'm with him. Even the crumbs from his table taste pretty good. I'm determined not to settle for less than I deserve. For the first time in my life I'm realizing that I deserve a lot. If it's meant to be, if he loves me a fraction of the amount I love him, he'll work it all out within himself and he'll be back. If not, I need to start learning now how to do without him."

"I guess you have it straight in your mind what's right for you," Jasmine said, sighing.

"Yes, I do. But, Jas, it still hurts so much."

She picked up the phone absentmindedly, her mind on the heavy subject the commentators were talking about on the Sunday afternoon news she and

Jasmine were watching after their conversation. "Hello."

"I haven't forgotten our brunch date." Steve's deep husky voice rumbled. "I can be over in a few minutes to pick you up."

Carmel started to demur. Then she realized she'd have to tell him her decision sometime. Now was a better time than any. "I'll meet you there. Was there anywhere in particular you wanted to eat?"

There was a hesitation at the other end of the line. "I thought you said you wanted to eat at the hotel we first . . ."

"Uh, yes. I forgot." She sure had. That wouldn't make delivering her news any easier, that was for certain. "I'll meet you there in an hour."

Carmel fingered the stem of her glass. She'd rushed to the hotel early to collect herself and strengthen her resolve.

"Carmel," Steve said. She flinched, startled. He'd come up behind her with that panther-like walk of his.

"Hi Steve." He made her feel shy and flushed. My God, he was a beautiful man.

"Have you ordered?" He perused the menu and a waiter appeared at his elbow. "I'll take the southern omelet," he said. "Whole wheat toast."

"I ate earlier with the family. I just want coffee," she said.

He grasped her hand and caressed her palm with his thumb. "I took the liberty of getting a room. Is that all right?"

She withdrew her hand. "We need to talk."

He arched an eyebrow.

Carmel cleared her throat. "I love being with you;

we have good times. But maybe you've noticed how hard I've been working on myself.''

"You seem less anxious, a little more accepting of your gorgeous body.''

"Thanks. I'm trying not to keep doing things that hurt me in the long run. Like using food to soothe jagged emotions or to keep me from facing what I feel.''

"All right. But what's your point, Carmel? You look serious.''

Men always wanted to get to the point. "Be patient. What I have to say isn't easy.''

"Go on.''

"It's about us. I don't think it's working.''

Steve's eyebrows shot up, surprise plain on his face. "I thought we worked very well together.''

"I'm not talking about sex. I'm talking about respect. I'm talking about the future. I'm talking about love.''

Steve swallowed and took a sip of water. The waiter appeared with their food and Steve relaxed, visibly grateful for the reprieve.

He picked up a fork and didn't meet her eyes. "What do you want from me, Carmel?''

"Apparently more than you're willing to give. And I've never been the settling type.''

"I've never asked you to settle for anything. I've been good to you. I thought I made you happy.''

"You do make me happy. But this goes to the root of my own self-esteem.''

"So what set this off? Is it because I was with Sienna last night? Hey, I can explain—''

Carmel raised a hand. "You don't need to explain. It has everything to do with you being with Sienna, but I doubt in the way you think. Listen to me. I want you to understand.''

She leaned forward, intense. "You have things to work out before we can truly be happy together. And you can't work them out with me; you've got to do it on your own. I've got my own stuff to do and I'm doing it. You need to do it too."

Steve was silent, but Carmel could feel the irritation building in him.

"I feel your ambivalence over being with a woman like me," she continued. "A woman my size. Let me be more specific, being with a woman my size in public display."

"That's not true."

"It is," Carmel said flatly. "That's one reason Sienna was sitting beside you last night instead of me. I don't know the other reasons, but you need to work on that, too. Your relationship with your ex-wife, especially if she's going to have your child, needs to be settled, boxed up and packed away before you start another one."

"I can explain."

"You don't need to explain," she said again. "I've made my decision."

"Carmel, calm down. Let's talk this over and you'll see that you're not making any sense . . ."

She looked at him sadly. "Did you hear anything I just said?"

"You're jealous of Sienna and you're mad I didn't ask you to the banquet."

"I suppose you could say that's the tip of the iceberg. You spend some time thinking about what I told you about the rest that's submerged, okay? I'm going to go. I'm really not hungry."

"Carmel? Don't do this."

"I've got to, Steve. Don't you see? It's starting to tear up the part I'm working so hard to heal. It's hurting me deep inside. I decided that the only thing

I need to settle for is the best, and if it hurts, it's not right for me. In the meantime, I'm not going anywhere. If you ever get things figured out, you know where to find me."

She started to rise. "So you're saying you don't care about me?" Steve asked.

"Not at all. The problem is that I care about you way, way too much." And she walked away before the tears stinging her eyes could fall.

Chapter 32

That feeling you have after someone punches you in the stomach? The one where you're bent over wanting to gasp in pain but can't because there's not that much breath left to draw? Steve pulled out of the hotel parking lot deciding that was close to how he was feeling right now.

Was it because he hated surprises? The wine Carmel poured over Sienna had amused him more than anything. Down inside he'd felt sort of pleased that his being with Sienna had disturbed her that much.

But now this. He still couldn't believe she'd dumped him. How dare she? Anger started to rise and it felt good, better than the despair and depression that had started to infuse him. And what in God's name was she talking about? She hadn't even given him a good reason. He could understand if he'd dogged her, but he'd treated her like a queen.

His thoughts continued in that vein until he pulled up into the garage of his house. He walked into the den where his father was reading the Sunday paper. "What's wrong with you?" Dad asked before he'd got into the room.

He ignored the question. "Where's Edna? I need to talk to her right now." Alarm shot through him. "She isn't gone, is she?" He hadn't realized how much he counted on talking with Carmel's mother until now. If she was gone, he didn't know what he'd do. He had no idea where she lived.

"She's in the kitchen."

Dad gave him a quizzical look at the relief he knew must have crossed his face.

He didn't stay to let Dad ask questions. He wheeled and went straight to the kitchen. Edna was standing at the counter chopping vegetables. She glanced up at him and smiled. "Have I ever told you how wonderful I think your kitchen is? I think I'd be happy spending most of my waking hours here."

"I've got to talk to you."

She glanced at him again and wiped her hands on her apron. "Fine. This has to do with my daughter, I assume?"

"You assume right. She just told me she doesn't want to see me again. I can't understand why. Things were going so well between us."

"Your father told me she threw a glass of wine on Sienna last night at a public function."

"More like she poured it."

"She must have been pissed to do that. You have no idea why?"

"Because I took Sienna and not her. And Sienna called her a fire truck. That didn't help."

"Ahhh. Was that the reason she gave you for the breakup? That you were with Sienna?"

"She said that it was the tip of the iceberg. She said I had work to do. She talked this craziness about how I felt about being with a big woman. Hell, I've shown her how I felt about being with her in living color more than once."

Then Steve cast a glance at Carmel's mother, embarrassed. "Sorry," he said.

"I see." There was a pause while Edna considered. "Shortly after my daughter met you she started dieting. She'd never done this seriously before. It was everything to her to lose weight. She couldn't do it."

Edna looked sideways at Steve. "Maybe I shouldn't be telling you this, but I am anyway. Carmel has always been the type of person who'd do whatever she put her mind to. Her body's necessity to maintain her setpoint weight was stronger. The failure devastated her. But, and this is the important part—listen up boy; it strengthened her, too. She went inside herself for the first time and that's where she is now. So, tell me, why did you take Sienna to that banquet?"

Steve shrugged. "It was nothing at the time. If I knew it would have been such a big deal I certainly wouldn't have. We'd just finished talking about something that upset her pretty badly, and my mother came in and suggested I take her. She wanted to go and—"

"See, that's what Carmel is talking about. She wanted to be by your side, and if you cared about her enough she would have been. You let your mom and other folks push you around too much because you don't have it straight in your head what you want.

"You need to straighten out this mess with that woman you were married to. You tell me she was upset, then you tell me she wanted to go to a party. Makes no sense. Carmel doesn't want to deal with that crap and I don't blame her. And last, but definitely not least, you need to go inside yourself and think about what you really want. I'll tell you what, my daughter isn't settling for any less than what she deserves, and that's to be number one all the way."

Steve stared at Edna, feeling stunned. Carmel's mother sure didn't mince words. Reminded him of Dad.

Monday was a hectic day at the office, but Steve was on automatic pilot. He couldn't get the situation with Carmel out of his mind. He still couldn't believe she'd dumped him like that when . . . when he needed her so much. He missed her with a sick feeling at the pit of his stomach already. But what was he going to do?

He returned to his office after his last patient, relieved the day was over, yet dreading going home to face another meal and an evening alone flipping through television channels.

He looked up to see his mother sitting behind his desk, and he suppressed a groan. He couldn't think of any person that he wanted to deal with less right now. "What's up, Mom?"

"I'm having a crisis and I need your help badly." Donna paused for dramatic effect.

Knowing his mother well, he sat in the comfortable chair next to his desk and waited for her to continue.

"Gene put me out. I had to call a moving company to get my things and put them in storage, and I'm at a hotel now. Oh God, Steven, I'm homeless."

He suppressed a frown of irritation. Mom had said her marriage had totally unraveled, the man was sleeping with another woman openly and had announced he didn't want her in his house. Now, was she telling him she didn't anticipate her husband's move? She should have moved out a long time ago. "Do you have money for an apartment?" he asked.

"Maybe for a deposit, but how am I going to pay monthly expenses? My credit cards alone . . ."

"How about getting a job?" he asked.

Silence.

She looked stunned, then horrified. "How could you suggest such a thing to me at this time?"

"Dad is not going to support you. Your reliance on him ended years ago. Your soon-to-be second ex-husband is not going to support you. Since you're way past twenty-one, I don't see your parents supporting you even if you were nice to them. I'll help, but I'm not going to support you either. I soon might have a family I need to provide for. So getting a job is your only option, the way I see it."

"I'm so pleased you took my advice and went out with Sienna. Wouldn't it be wonderful if you two got back together?" Donna said, totally ignoring what he said about getting a job.

"There is no way on God's green earth that I'm going to get back with Sienna. The first time was bad enough."

"But she's going to have your child and my grand-baby."

"No, she isn't. I took her out not because you advised it, but out of sheer relief."

"You lying," Donna said flatly. "I spoke to her just the other day. If something had happened to the baby, I'd be the first to know."

"Stop deluding yourself, Mom. Sienna doesn't give a damn about anyone but herself. She reminds me of you."

His mother's face crumpled. He felt guilty. But everything he said was true and one day his mother was going to have to face the truth. He handed her a box of tissues.

"Why are you telling me these lies about Sienna?

Why don't you do what I want for a change? All I want is to be a grandmother to my grandchild and you want to withhold that from me, too."

There was a snap within him and a surge of anger rushed up. "I said Sienna isn't pregnant. The details behind her actions are rather sordid, but that's nothing new to me. Did I ever give you the details behind our breakup? She was sleeping with a friend of mine and I caught them. It wasn't out of any great passion either, just out of what she thought he could do for her. Sienna is nothing but a whore, an expensive one, but a whore nevertheless." He turned a hard eye on his mother. "That could be another word for somebody who continually expects some man's support rather than standing on her own two feet. Get a job."

His mother got up out of the chair. She walked to the office window and looked out onto the parking lot. "Is there anything else you have to say to me?" she asked quietly.

"One more thing. When I talked about marriage and family, I was talking about Carmel Matthews. Out of all the women I've met, she has by far the most love inside. She's beautiful, soft and womanly and I didn't fully accept her even though I loved her."

Donna folded her arms across her chest and dropped her head, but she didn't speak.

"I was too worried about what people would think. I may have lost her because I've been acting and feeling too much like you. Like mother, like son, huh? But no more. I reject everything you stand for. And do you know what else? I'm going to do whatever it takes to get her back. And that includes her family. Oh, by the way, her mother and Dad seem to have really hit it off. If you want to have any part at all in our lives in the future, I suggest you get used to the way it's going to be. I plan to call Carmel and beg for her forgiveness as soon as I get home."

Suddenly his mother looked old and fragile and in pain beyond what she ever previously comprehended. She nodded. "Everything I have done has been wrong. Everything I do is a mistake. You're right, of course. The only thing that matters anymore is your happiness." She turned back to the window. "I feel too hopeless to go on living, but I don't know how to end it." She paused. "But I'll figure it out."

Her words were soft and utterly sincere. For once his mother's voice had not a trace of blame or drama-mongering in it.

"Mom, you will always have me and you could have family whom you love and who love you just as much back. I think some changes could be the beginning of hope for you."

He put an arm around her shoulders. "Come on. I have this place I want you to go and see what you think. I want you to be safe, and you need a quiet space to think about those changes I just mentioned. There's a good hospital I know where you can take the time to think and heal. I think it'll make all the difference in the world to you, Mom." He picked up her jacket and draped it over her shoulders and picked up her purse. His mother didn't protest as he led her gently from the room.

The house was still and quiet when Steve finally returned home. Dad must have gone to bed early. Steve's hard words to his mother had proved to be a turning point for her. She was willing to get the help she needed and he prayed that one day she'd be able to be truly happy.

He sat behind the desk in his office and stared at

the phone. It was late but he needed to call Carmel. He needed to set things right between them. He needed her. She'd simply been upset about seeing Sienna and him together. Once she understood what happened everything would be all right.

He picked up the phone and dialed. She answered on the second ring. "Carmel, I never told you what happened with Sienna. That's what this is really all about, isn't it?"

He heard her quiet sigh.

"No, it's not what this is all about," she said. "I don't care—"

"Just listen to me, Carmel. Do me a favor and just listen. I confronted Sienna the other night with some news I'd obtained yesterday, and she recanted. She's not four months pregnant by me. She was barely eight weeks pregnant by her married boss." He paused, waiting for her reaction.

"I'm sure that's a relief," she said, her tone emotionless.

Steve frowned, disappointed. "She tried to use the pregnancy to get him to leave his wife and it backfired badly," he continued. "She no longer has a job either. It'll be announced as a resignation, but she's been fired. She had to clear out her desk over a week ago."

He waited and emptiness stretched out between them. Starting to feel nervous, he wondered why she wasn't saying anything. He'd expected her to be excited and exclaiming over how happy she was to hear the news.

"Sienna lied to me because she wanted my support when she saw the way the wind was blowing. She saw an opportunity because of the stupid thing I did months ago and she took it. Her biological clock is ticking. She thought she could have the baby and pass it off as mine."

Carmel said nothing. Anxiety built within him.

"But I'd told her there was no way that we were getting back together, baby or not, and she made a last-ditch effort to force her boss to leave his wife. That's what got her fired. What do you think of that?"

"Not much," Carmel said.

"She's no longer pregnant either. She went ahead and had an abortion right after she was canned."

He was talking too fast and too much. He wished she would say something.

"Why don't you say something?" he asked her, frustration in his voice.

"I said all I needed to say this morning. I'm pleased for you though. It definitely makes your life less complicated. Good-bye, now." Then she hung up. Just like that.

Steve sat listening to the dead air on the line feeling disbelief and fear. No. He couldn't have lost her, right when he realized how special she was to him.

Chapter 33

Loneliness. Carmel raised her head and looked out at the deepening blue of twilight from her front porch. She opened herself to the feeling, let it pass through her. Maybe she needed to take a class or something in the evenings. Get out and meet some people. Make a new girlfriend or two.

The thought of any man other than Steve was still a little too much to bear. Days had melded to weeks. Jasmine left, Mama was around much less due to the interest she and Marvin found in each other.

Carmel kept on with her life. She'd found a job in home health, nurtured her children and worked through issues with Melanie. She used the newly free stretches of time to work on herself, but she missed the people who used to share her life. Especially Steve. His loss still felt as if someone had torn out her heart and left a hole. A day didn't go by when she didn't worry that she'd made a terrible mistake by letting him go, and she'd have to reassure herself that she didn't.

"Mom, you still there?" Melanie stuck her head out the door and asked for the tenth time.

"Yes, hon. What's up? Why are you so worried that I'm going to go anywhere?"

A low-slung white car pulled up. It was Jasmine's new car, and Carmel stood up, excited. Jas had said nothing about driving up.

"You look great," Jasmine breathed after they hugged.

"And I haven't lost an ounce," Carmel said. "Everyone asks me how much weight have I lost and what diet am I on. I haven't dieted a minute. I just changed my style and lost a couple of dress sizes with my exercise, that's all. I do feel great though."

"You look it."

"So do you. How's that man treating you?"

Jasmine's lips tightened. "I've got a surprise for you," she said, not responding to Carmel's question.

"What's that?" Carmel asked, grinning, happy enough to see her friend and willing to let the man thing go for now.

"Tickets to the Falcons' playoff game."

"No, you didn't. Those are impossible to get."

"Impossible or not, I not only got two for the both of us, I got two more for Trey and Melanie. I got them on short notice and the game is going to start now, so hurry up."

Carmen frowned. "I think that game already started."

"Nope. Hurry up, change into something stunning."

"To go see a football game that we'll be lucky to get to by halftime? I appreciate the sentiment, not to mention the difficulty of getting tickets, but football, Jas? We don't even like football.''

"Melanie," Jasmine called. "Help me out here. Your mother is balking.''

"Mom, come on and hurry up. I want to go.''

The crowd was in a frenzy when they got there. The score was close and it seemed to be some sort of critical moment in the game. Carmel had even less of a clue about what was going on in football than in baseball, but she was impressed by the seats. Right out near the field on the fifty-yard line. She wasn't sure, but she thought those were pretty good seats. She wondered how in heaven's name did Jasmine get the tickets.

"Carmel!'' came from behind her. Her eyes widened to see Marvin and Mama sitting a row behind them. She waved at them. My goodness, what was up? She remembered Mama saying something about how football was a substitute for war and she wasn't going to subsidize a bunch of overgrown men trying to kill each other. Mama didn't think much of football.

Carmel pondered the significance of all this until finally it was time for the halftime show.

She looked up to see the scoreboard flashing the words, "Steve Reynolds Loves Carmel Matthews!''

She blinked and looked again, sure she was experiencing a hallucination. Nope, there it was. Could there be another two people with the same names?

Now the board was flashing, "Will You Marry Me?''

Before she could absorb this, Trey yelled, "Look over there, Mom.'' Carmel looked and about had a heart attack.

There she was on the huge television monitors hanging in the stadium. There Steve was walking toward her. Then the sports announcer's voice echoed through the stadium. "Dr. Steve Reynolds declares his love and honorable intentions in front of God, the Atlanta Falcons and seventy thousand people in the stadium. Will you marry him?"

And he was in front of her, reaching her. She no longer cared about the television monitors because once he took her in his arms, he smelled and felt so good, she wanted to cry and laugh at the same time.

Then he pulled away and dropped on his knees and took her hand. He took out a ring with a simple gold band and a brilliant large diamond that glittered and sparkled in the stadium lights, and he slid it on the fourth finger of her left hand. The crowd roared.

"I love you Carmel and I can't live without you. I wanted to let you know at a public function, and I couldn't think of anything more public than this."

Mama, Marvin, Jasmine and Carmel's children beamed. The bands of the halftime show had begun marching, and Steve drew her in his arms again. "Let's get out of here," Steve whispered in her ear.

Carmel nodded, wondering if life got any better than this.

Of course it did. She knew in her heart that was only the beginning of their very long and happy ever after.

Dear Reader,

I hope you enjoyed Carmel's journey to self-acceptance and love. I believe almost every woman will identify to some degree with the heroine's struggle to accept her body despite societal expectations. I haven't seen many romances with a heroine Carmel's size or that frankly tackle the issue of weight and body acceptance. It wasn't an easy book for me to write, but I felt that this was a story that needed to be told. Love comes in all sizes and shapes as well as colors.

Visit me at *http://www.comports.com/monica*. I'd love to hear what you think about the issues I raised in this book and how it affected you. Write me at *Monica@comports.com* or P.O. Box 654, Topeka, KS 66601.

Good reading,
Monica Jackson

THESE ARABESQUE ROMANCES
ARE NOW MOVIES FROM BET!